FORT LEE PUBLIC LIBRARY, NJ
3 9117 09036084 0

W9-ALJ-966

DATE DUE
12/22/03

RETURN
TO THE
ISLAND

ALSO BY GLORIA WHELAN

THE ISLAND TRILOGY

ONCE ON THIS ISLAND
Book One

FAREWELL TO THE ISLAND
Book Two

• • •

HOMELESS BIRD

THE INDIAN SCHOOL

MIRANDA'S LAST STAND

GLORIA WHELAN

HarperCollins*Publishers*

Return to the Island

Printed in the United States of America. For information address HarperCollins Children's Books, a division of HarperCollins Publishers, 1350 Avenue of the Americas, New York, NY 10019.
www.harperchildrens.com

Library of Congress Cataloging-in-Publication Data
Whelan, Gloria.
Return to the island / Gloria Whelan.
p. cm.
Summary: In 1818 Mary O'Shea must decide whether to remain on Michilimackinac Island and marry her dear Indian friend White Hawk or to accept the proposal of James, an English nobleman, and to go with him to London.
ISBN 0-06-028253-3 — ISBN 0-06-028254-1 (lib. bdg.)
[1. Mackinac Island (Mich.)—Fiction. 2. Indians of North America—Michigan—Fiction. 3. Frontier and pioneer life—Michigan—Fiction. 4. Michigan—History—To 1837—Fiction.] I. Title.
PZ7.W5718 Re 2000 00-29575
[Fic]—dc21 CIP
AC

Typography by Christine Kettner
1 2 3 4 5 6 7 8 9 10
❖
First Edition

For Gloria and Don

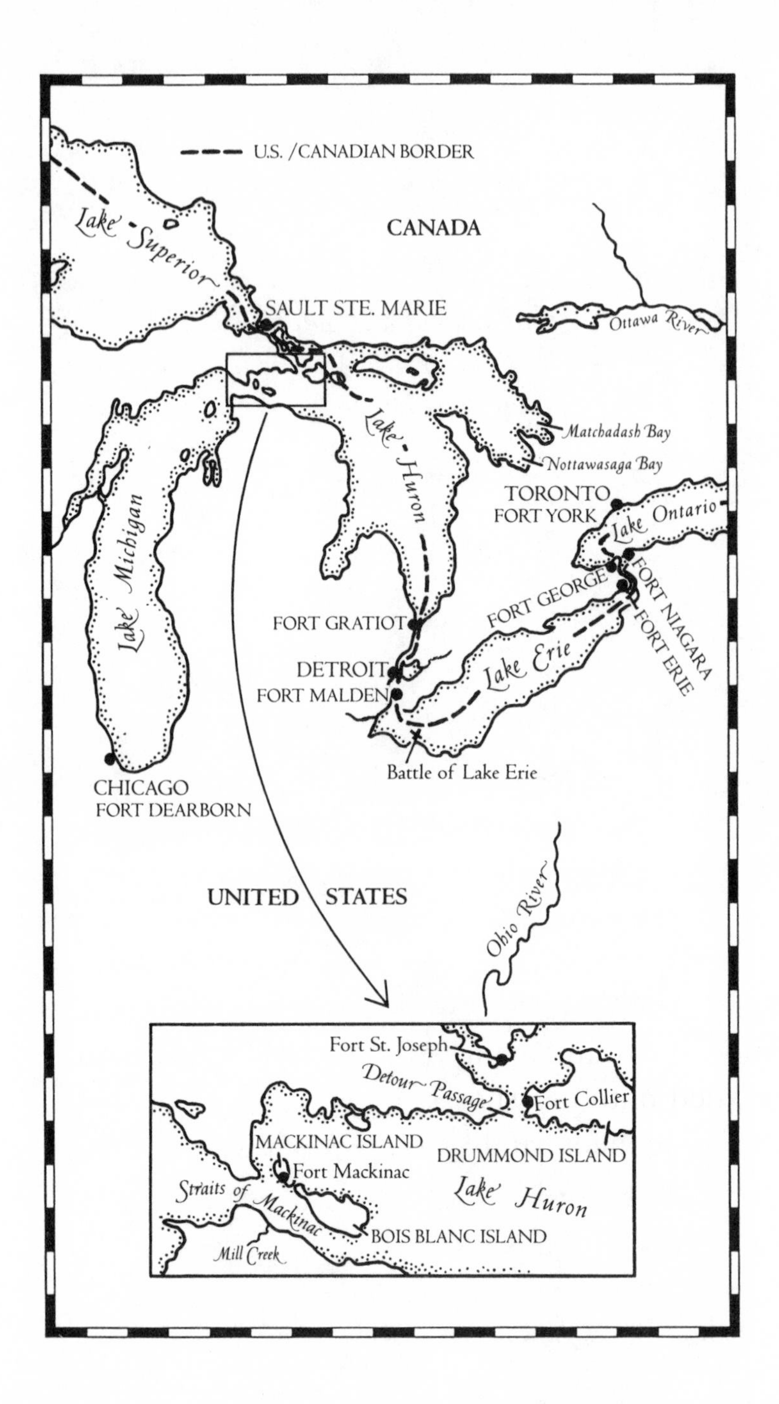
U.S. /CANADIAN BORDER
CANADA
Lake Superior
SAULT STE. MARIE
Ottawa River
Lake Huron
Matchadash Bay
Nottawasaga Bay
TORONTO
FORT YORK
Lake Ontario
Lake Michigan
FORT GEORGE
FORT NIAGARA
FORT ERIE
FORT GRATIOT
DETROIT
FORT MALDEN
Lake Erie
Battle of Lake Erie
CHICAGO
FORT DEARBORN
UNITED STATES
Ohio River
Fort St. Joseph
Detour Passage
Fort Collier
MACKINAC ISLAND
DRUMMOND ISLAND
Fort Mackinac
Straits of Mackinac
Lake Huron
BOIS BLANC ISLAND
Mill Creek

CHAPTER

1

OUR ISLAND OF MICHILIMACKINAC had never been more alive. White-winged schooners flew in and out of the harbor. Fishermen set their nets at dawn and were back at twilight with their catch. The heartbeat of the Indian drums sounded day and night. A thousand Indians were crowded onto our shores. I could make out the Ottawa teepees, and those of the Ojibwa, and the Potawatomi. The smoke from their camp-fires rose and mingled with the low clouds that hung over Michilimackinac. Many of the Indians were there to receive a yearly payment in exchange for having given their land to our government. But some of them were still loyal to the British. Each spring they camped here on their way to Canada, where the British kept their friendship with generous gifts. In the fall, on their way home, the same Indians would stop on the island once again, proudly showing off jackets of fine British broadcloth and arms ringed round with gifts of silver.

The *voyageurs* were arriving from the east, their *bateaux* loaded with trade goods, their red caps and sashes bright as a cardinal's feather, their French songs drowning out the cries of the gulls. Day after day the brigades of traders returned to the island with stories of lands farther north than Superior and farther west than the great Mississippi. Their pelts were weighed and baled, put on cargo canoes, and sent down Lake Huron and across Lake Erie to Buffalo. From Buffalo the furs traveled by wagon to Albany, then once again by boat down the Hudson to New York and then across the sea. It was a journey I had made myself only two years before when I had visited my sister, Angelique, in London.

Beyond the crowded, noisy town, the rest of Mackinac Island was unchanged. The waves still argued with the rocky shore. Forests of spruce and cedar huddled together to shut out the sunlight. The rackety eagles' nest that White Hawk had discovered in the crown of a tall pine was still there.

From my perch at the edge of our farm I looked out at Lake Michigan to the west and Lake Huron to the east. In the sun their waters shone like endless bolts of blue and green silk. It was here that we had buried Papa. The lilac bush I had planted beside his grave was bursting into bloom. Papa, who had slipped away in the autumn with no more fuss or struggle than the gentle falling of a leaf, lay beside Mama. Their gravestones read: *Annette Duclouis O'Shea, born Beauvais, France, June 1774, died Michilimackinac, March 1800. Matthew O'Shea, born County Wicklow, Ireland, April 1768, died Michilimackinac, November 1817.* Mama had to flee France because her family had supported the French king, while Papa had to escape from Ireland because his family had opposed the English king. Now my sister, Angelique, was married to a British man, Daniel Cunningham, and living in England with him and their nine-month-old son, Matthew.

The only family I had on the island was my brother, Jacques, his wife, Little Cloud, and their son, Renard.

Before she had married and left the island Angelique had planted primroses and lilies of the valley around Mama's grave. These May flowers were blooming now, the primroses in bright yellow and purple, the lilies of the valley sending up their fragrance. Mama had died the year I was born. All I had of her was a box of her recipes and her silver cross. I had sent Angelique the miniature portrait of Mama that Papa carried always. Papa had been everything to me. He had left me the farm when he died. All winter long the farm had been asleep. Now, with the spring planting, I hardly knew which way to turn, and I certainly had no business dawdling about and thinking idle thoughts.

The idle thoughts were swept away when Little Cloud came running toward me, long braids flying, Renard's cradleboard bouncing on her back. "Come quick, Mary! Jacques and Mr. Astor's bad man! They are killing one another!"

Together we flew down the path to the village, slipping on the sand and tearing our skirts on the briars. Shouts were coming from Market Street. We ran past the row of whitewashed houses, safe behind their picket fences. There in front of the American Fur Company office I was horrified to see my brother, Jacques, rolling around in the dust of the street with Mr. Brandson. There was no killing. The two men were hanging on to one another so tightly they hardly knew whose body to pound. The door of the office swung open, and two clerks ran out. While Little Cloud and I tugged at Jacques, the clerks pulled at Mr. Brandson. Little Cloud and I landed on our bottoms with Jacques on top of us, while Mr. Brandson was caged in the arms of the clerks.

"Jacques! What can you be thinking of to brawl in the streets like some ruffian!" In my anger and shame I felt tears stinging my eyes.

"You'll never be a fur trader again!" Mr. Brandson shouted. "I'll see no company ever buys another pelt from you." His hands were doubled into fists. Since Mr. Astor had put this large, loud man in command of the American Fur Company, Mr. Brandson had strutted about town like the only rooster in the yard. But now, as I watched him brush the dust from his clothes and head for the office, my shame dissolved. I had to bite my lip to keep from laughing. Though he tried to look dignified, he was limping along on one shoe, and a rip in the back of his trousers revealed a large patch of flannel drawers.

Jacques had to have the last word. He called out, "You're a thief and a bully, Brandson!"

Half the town had gathered to witness the fight. From the corner of my eye I saw a shocked-looking Mrs. West and her daughter Elizabeth. Her other daughter, Emma, was hurrying toward us. "Mary, you and Little Cloud and the baby must come and tidy up." She brushed the dust from my skirt and put Renard's cradleboard to rights on Little Cloud's back.

"I have to see to Jacques," I said. Blood was flowing from a cut on his forehead.

"He must come too. Papa will see to him. I'll settle things with Mama."

The three of us made a sad parade of it as we trailed along behind Emma. She spoke briefly to Mrs. West and Elizabeth. Their eyebrows shot up, but when they saw that Jacques needed Dr. West's care, they gave a great sigh and, noses in the air, followed us down the street to their house.

Dr. West was the physician for the soldiers at the fort as well as the island's doctor. His home, unlike my simple cabin, was handsome and well appointed. There were Turkey rugs on the floors and silk curtains at the windows. The walls of the sitting room had been papered over so that only the bumps beneath the flowered paper gave away a house of logs. Meals were served on a fine mahogany table ordered from England. Two silver candlesticks rested on the table. Mrs. West always said they had been handed down in her family, but it was secretly told the candlesticks had been given to Dr. West by a patient grateful to be cured of the gout. The patient was Colonel McDouall, who had been the commander of the fort when the British occupied the island during the three years of war between America and England.

Mrs. West winced as Jacques entered the house. While Little Cloud and I were sensible of her fine furniture, Jacques crashed through the room like a moose through the underbrush.

As Dr. West attended the cut on Jacques's forehead, Mrs. West scolded, "What were you thinking of, Jacques, to get into a common brawl with Mr. Brandson? Surely you know how important he is in the American Fur Company. You will never work for Mr. Astor again." Before he became an independent trader, Jacques had been a clerk for the company.

"I would rather be cut up into a million pieces than work for that thief!"

The angry tone of his father's voice set Renard to crying. Even Dr. West looked shocked. Mrs. West and Elizabeth nearly fainted. Since Mr. Astor had brought the American Fur Company to Michilimackinac, the island had prospered. His clerks, and Mr. Brandson and his other managers, had built homes here. We now had dances and teas. If you were like Emma and Elizabeth and didn't have to hoe fields and muck out a barn as I did, you could put on a party dress every night in the week. Elizabeth said, "How can you say such things against Mr. Astor? He has made the island civilized, and Mr. Brandson is a gentleman. I'm sure he would never have engaged in a fight unless he was sorely provoked." It was well known that Elizabeth was setting her cap for Mr. Brandson.

Jacques reached for Renard, lifting his crying baby out of the cradle on Little Cloud's back. As he dandled his son to cheer him, Jacques said, "Brandson is no gentleman. He is nothing more than a thief. Little Cloud's father, Chief Black Wolf, agreed to sell his tribe's pelts to me because I gave him a better price than Astor's company did. Brandson sent thugs from the

American Fur Company to threaten the chief. They told him they had influence with the government, warning him that the great white father would take all his lands if they traded with me. An independent trader doesn't have a chance against Astor and his men. He destroys their camps and burns their canoes. Astor thinks he owns every four-footed animal that walks the earth."

Dr. West said, "Be still, Jacques, while I put in a couple of stitches. Emma, perhaps you could give Jacques a glass of brandy to steady him."

Mrs. West poured a very small measure into a crystal glass and reluctantly handed the delicate glass to Emma. As Emma offered it to Jacques, she looked at him tenderly with her large brown eyes. Before his marriage to Little Cloud, Emma had been very fond of Jacques. Now, though she was still fond of him, she had given up all hope. Who could pine for a man with a nine-month-old baby spitting up on him?

Jacques handed Renard back to Little Cloud. The baby's name had been a compromise. Little Cloud wanted to call him Red Fox, because his hair was red like mine, but Jacques wanted a French name. Jacques called the baby Renard, which is French for fox, but Little Cloud still called him Red Fox.

Jacques was brave during the stitching. Emma, Elizabeth, and their mother covered their eyes. I have to admit I looked away, but Little Cloud never flinched. When it was over, Dr. West had some advice for Jacques. "You are a married man and a father, Jacques. It's time for you to make a home. You can't continue to disappear into the wilds each fall. Your father is gone now. Why don't you settle down with your family on the farm and give Mary a hand?"

I winced. It was true I was sorely in need of help with the farm Papa had left to me, but I knew how independent Jacques was. He wanted things his way or no way at all. He would never be happy working someone else's farm, not even mine. I wanted my brother and his wife and son nearby, but not so close as all that.

Dr. West must have seen the troubled look on my face. He said no more about Jacques's helping me, but made an excellent suggestion. "Charlotte Sinclair told me only last week that since her husband died she longs to join her sister in Detroit. If you could offer a fair price for her farm, I am sure she would take it. Since it is next to Mary's farm, and since it is small, requiring little work, you could still give Mary a hand when it was needed."

"What about White Hawk?" Jacques asked. "Don't you think that as the Sinclairs' adopted son he might want the farm?"

Dr. West shook his head. "He is often with his mother, helping her with the farm, but you know yourself he is not ready to settle down. When he's not with his tribe at L'Arbre Croche, or here on the island, he's in Detroit. Mrs. Sinclair would see him there. I am sure White Hawk would be pleased to have the farm go to you, Jacques."

Jacques looked at Little Cloud. "What do you say?"

She smiled. "It would be well for Red Fox to live on land of his own. My people may not be so lucky." Little Cloud's father, Chief Black Wolf, and his Sauk tribe were seeing more and more of their land taken over by settlers. The settlers were like hungry dogs nibbling away, first on one bit and then on another.

I eagerly agreed. "I think it's an excellent idea." Little Cloud was a better farmer than Jacques, and I was sure that if he listened to her they might succeed on the Sinclair farm. With my sister, Angelique, in London and Papa gone, I longed to keep what was left of our small family on the island. The Sinclair farm was next to mine, and it would be a joy to have Jacques, Little Cloud, and Renard as neighbors.

Jacques jumped up from his chair, paying no mind to his injury and nearly upsetting a delicate china shepherd on a table. "I'll see Mrs. Sinclair this afternoon," he said. "In fact I'll do it right now!" He dashed from the room, pausing only to fling a word of thanks to the Wests. No one was surprised at his rash behavior. Jacques is wholehearted. When an idea comes into his head, it crowds out everything else. On his way out he nearly knocked over Pere Mercier.

The priest put himself to rights and cautiously settled his ample frame on the edge of one of Mrs. West's fragile chairs. I noticed Pere Mercier's cassock was wet about its edges. That and a sunburned nose were sure signs he had been out in his boat, fishing. His excuse for spending long hours in his boat was that the apostles were fishermen.

Now he shook his head. "Jacques was ever one to cut a knot instead of untying it," he said. "He's made an enemy for life of Brandson."

Worried, I asked, "Can Mr. Brandson do Jacques harm?"

"Perhaps not, Mary," Pere Mercier said, "but

this is a small island. There is no pleasure in coming face-to-face with your enemy every day of your life." He gave me a gentle smile. "I didn't come to scold. I have good news. I was out in my boat when I saw White Hawk's canoe heading this way from L'Arbre Croche. He's probably already on the island. Never was a son more attentive to his mother."

I'm afraid I was clumsy in my haste to make my excuses to the Wests. I know I could not hide my blushes and my eagerness.

A moment later I was racing up the hill to our farm as quickly as I had hurried down the path to town only an hour before. This time I was not hastening toward some feared killing, but toward White Hawk, my dearest friend in all the world.

CHAPTER

As I BURST INTO my cabin, the sun was streaming through the blue-and-yellow calico curtains. There was the friendly smell of rising bread mingled with the fragrance of bunches of dried rosemary and lavender. A yellow-and-blue quilt Angelique and I had made together was spread over my cot. Papa's Brown Bess musket hung over the stone fireplace Papa had fashioned from the boulders that shouldered their way up on the island. I had used the musket only the day before to bring down a pair of grouse for the stew pot. Visiting the Wests' elegant house always made me rejoice in my own modest home.

I knew White Hawk would stop in, as he always did on his way to see his mother, Mrs. Sinclair. As a child White Hawk had been rescued in a Lake Michigan storm by Mr. Sinclair. White Hawk's parents had drowned in the storm, so the Sinclairs had raised him. It was only when he was fifteen that White Hawk had discovered his father had been an Ottawa chief at the nearby village, L'Arbre Croche. Now he was often with his tribe. I knew his heart was torn. I saw how tender White Hawk was to his mother and how hard he worked to keep the farm just as she liked it, yet his Ottawa people were also in his heart.

Since my return from London, I had spent much time in White Hawk's company. Though we took the same delight we always had in coming upon a hidden patch of wild strawberries and in climbing the bluffs for a fine view of the lakes, things were not quite as they had been. In the past, I had scrambled over the rocks and climbed trees with no thought for how I looked. Now I was ever aware of White Hawk's presence and of what he must think of me. Often I caught him watching me, and when I gave him my hand so he could help me climb a steep cliff, he was not quick to release it.

Hastily I poured water out of the pitcher into the washbasin and splashed my face. I pinned up my straight red hair, wishing for the thousandth time I had Angelique's black ringlets. I had just kicked off my muddy boots and was reaching under the bed, hunting for my shoes, when White Hawk walked through the door.

"You needn't try to hide from me, Mary." He was laughing.

There was that second's hesitation that comes when two friends who have been apart look for some signal that all is still well between them. I was reassured by White Hawk's smile and hurried to greet him. He was dressed in his usual fashion, in corduroy trousers and fringed deerskin jacket. Two thick black braids hung down beneath his wide-brimmed hat. He had hooded black eyes and high cheekbones, and his smile always suggested that he was enjoying some secret. These last months he had grown sturdier, more a man and less the boy with whom I had climbed trees and picked berries.

White Hawk held on to my hand and turned me about. "Well, Mary, I see you are dressed in the height of fashion, with matching holes in your stockings, dirt under your nails, and bloodstains on your dress. I heard about Jacques and Brandson." His face clouded over. "I only wish I had been there to join in the pummeling Brandson received. That man is no friend of the Indian."

"However much you may dislike Mr. Brandson, White Hawk, I know you too well to think you would roll about in the street as Jacques did."

"Perhaps you're right. There are other ways of dealing with Astor and his henchmen. If we Indians would just band together, we would be the ones with power instead of the American Fur Company." He sighed. "But that's an impossible wish. Tecumseh spent a lifetime traveling the country to bring the Indians together and never succeeded. I can't even get the chiefs of my own tribe at L'Arbre Croche to agree."

"How long will you stay on the island?" I asked, hoping the answer would be "several weeks," but knowing better.

"Only long enough to help Mother with the farm. I wish it were longer, Mary." He looked at me as if there were more he wished to say, but after a moment he only sighed and added, "The farm is too much for my mother. What she really wants is to sell it and live with her sister in Detroit."

The door flew open, and Jacques rushed into the house with Little Cloud trailing behind him. He clasped White Hawk on the shoulder and said, "If you say yes, it's all settled." Jacques pounded White Hawk on the back by way of a friendly greeting. "I left your mother not five minutes ago, and we agreed on a price for the farm. In spite of Astor's trying to ruin me, I did well selling my pelts. Anyhow, you're no farmer. Even if you know the Latin names of plants, you don't know how to make them grow."

Jacques was only joking. No one worked harder than White Hawk or took more pleasure in a fat cabbage or a new piglet.

"That's excellent news, Jacques." White Hawk looked relieved. "I am in no position to take over the farm, and there is no one I would rather see there. As to making plants grow, thank heavens you'll have Little Cloud to tell you what to do. Now I'm off to see Mother, but I promise to come back this evening for a reunion."

Jacques spent the afternoon stalking about the cabin, too excited to sit still. He made extravagant plans for his new farm, plans more suitable to a great estate than to a few acres of stony soil. Little Cloud was as enthusiastic as Jacques, but her plans were more sensible. "It is just the time to begin to sprout squash seeds," she said. "We'll wrap them in a bundle of fur and grasses and hang them next to the fireplace. There they will stay warm in the cool spring evenings. A little water each day will keep them moist. In a few days we will have sprouts to plant." Her handsome face lit up. "This summer there will be squash blossoms to cook."

"Squash blossoms to cook?" I had never heard of such a thing.

"They are so good. I boil them with a bit of fat." Little Cloud licked her lips. "I can taste them now."

Jacques said, "I'll leave the eating of flowers to you. For myself, I'm going to plant an orchard of apple and pear trees. And we must have a pig or two."

"Belle's new calf will be yours," I said. "You'll have milk for Renard, so he'll grow up sturdy and strong."

Jacques frowned. "I don't see how he can be sturdy and strong if Little Cloud keeps him bundled up on her back all day in that cradleboard."

"It is good for him to be with me," Little Cloud insisted. "If he is hungry, there I am. If he worries, I am there as well."

Jacques and Little Cloud often argued in this way about the raising of their son. Little Cloud wished to raise him as the children of her people were raised. Jacques had other ideas. Only the day before, Jacques had complained that Little Cloud was always pulling the end of Renard's nose. "A long nose is a sign of beauty," Little Cloud said.

"Not to my way of thinking," Jacques said. Now they were quarreling again. To end the argument I sent Jacques out for firewood and engaged Little Cloud in helping me scale the whitefish Pere Mercier had given us for our supper, happy in the thought that my small family would be living nearby.

White Hawk was as good as his word, and our gathering that evening was most amiable. The May evening was chilly, and a cheery fire burned on the hearth. Renard fell asleep after White Hawk made many admiring remarks on his appearance and on the strength in his little fingers as he grasped White Hawk's thumb. Jacques, Little Cloud, White Hawk, and myself spent the rest of the evening telling stories. Of course Jacques went first, for nothing ever held him back.

He loved to tell how he had set out with his four *engagés*, men he had hired to portage the canoe around waterfalls and through heavy brush. They had left Michilimackinac with a canoe full of trade goods: silver, earbobs, bracelets, blankets, bolts of calico, kettles, traps, and guns. Little by little, as they traveled west, the trade goods were exchanged for pelts. I was glad for Jacques's success, but I mourned for all the small creatures sacrificed for their pelts. I saw the same sad look on White Hawk's face. The two of us often stood silently by the lake or deep in the woods, delighted to see those same animals wild and free.

"Astor's men are everywhere," Jacques complained. "When they can't win over the Indians by offering more trade goods than the independent traders offer, they threaten the Indians or beat up the independents. If you think today's fight with Brandson was anything, you should have seen me take on his bullies in the woods.

"We managed to do better than Astor's men, because we worked harder: sheltering from the rain at night under a tarpaulin, up early in the morning and still paddling late at night. Once we traveled sixty-eight miles in a single day, with nothing to eat but lyed corn and bear grease." Jacques spoke of the herds of buffalo. "In the wintertime the beasts are covered with snow. They look like great white humps. Their muzzles are covered with hoarfrost, and icicles hang from their chins. You see a hundred beasts all facing into the wind or rooting with their noses for grass under the snow."

Jacques had fearful tales as well. He told stories of unfriendly Indian tribes, mosquitoes so numerous that they got into your ears and nose so that you couldn't breathe, and rattlesnakes dropping from trees.

The rattlesnake story caused Little Cloud to cover her face and giggle. "No, Jacques. Never from trees!" she said. The country Jacques was describing had been her country. When he spoke of the endless prairie, I had seen tears come to her eyes, for she missed her village of Saukenuk. Jacques had met Little Cloud two years before, when he was trading for furs in her village. Her home was here now, but a part of her heart was still with her people. She joined eagerly in his descriptions of her village.

"You have never seen so pretty a place,"

Little Cloud said. "We have the wild Rock River on one side and the great father of rivers on the other. The earth does not spit up stones as it does here on the island. Everywhere you look there are fields of thick green grass, soft as the curtains in the Wests' house. In the spring it seems that every bird in the world follows the father of rivers north. In the fall we see the birds fly south. They are so many, the whole sky beats like a feathered wing. Our kettles are always filled with rabbit and deer meat."

"There are no better hunters than your people," Jacques agreed. "Your father tried to talk the other chiefs into trading their pelts with me as he had done. Unfortunately, Astor's men encouraged the other chiefs to borrow money from his company to buy their trade goods. They have become more and more indebted to Astor, and now they're prisoners of the company. That's not the worst of it. The Secretary of War has sent an agent to Little Cloud's people to talk them into selling their land and moving west."

Little Cloud said, "How can I think of my village if it is no longer there? And what of our son? When Red Fox becomes a man and wishes to see the land of his people, will he find a white man's town instead?"

"Even though Little Cloud's father is against selling," Jacques said, "there are other chiefs who are tempted by the large annuities that are offered them."

As he listened White Hawk grew angrier and angrier. In the light of the fire his dark eyes flashed. "It's the same here. Even our own chiefs at L'Arbre Croche argue among themselves over the selling of our land. When I was down in Detroit, I heard Governor Cass was trying to get the land around the Saginaw Bay away from the Chippewas." The anger left his face and he laughed. "Can you believe that when I was down there Pere Richard asked me to teach Latin in his new university?"

The Sinclairs had seen to White Hawk's education. As soon as he could read he began to study Latin with Pere Mercier. He became the priest's star pupil. It was always a sorrow to me that there was no school on the island, and Pere Mercier did not teach girls. My only learning had come in the hours Angelique had spent teaching me.

"You aren't going to Detroit, are you?" I asked. I didn't want White Hawk to be hundreds of miles away.

"Never. Can you imagine me locked into a

stuffy room teaching bored young men to decline irregular verbs? Still, I must go down to Detroit from time to time. If I am to be of any help to my people, I must know what plots the government there is hatching."

The fire had died down. A full moon shone through the window. "It's past midnight," White Hawk said. "Mother will be worried." He turned to me. "Will you walk a bit with me, Mary? It's as bright as day out, and you know the path."

I had walked that path a thousand times. Eagerly I jumped up and followed White Hawk outside. We could see the Indian campfires below us. The drums were still throbbing. The full moon silvered our way. Fireflies were tangled like fallen stars in the grasses. An owl hooted. Just ahead of us some small animal darted into the brush. We could sense the soft swooping of bats. Night made the familiar path seem like a strange country.

White Hawk reached for my hand. More than his height and the broadness of his shoulders, the strength of his grasp told me that he was now a man. "I only wanted to have you to myself for a moment, Mary," he said. "Jacques would talk the sun up and down. I was hoping you and I could take a few hours tomorrow and wander over the island as we used to do. We're no longer children, but surely we're entitled to some pleasure. We could explore the cave or climb Arch Rock."

Arch Rock was a bridge of stone rising over a hundred feet from the water. I remembered White Hawk telling me its Ottawa legend. A young woman, She-Who-Walks-in-the-Mist, met a handsome brave. They fell deeply in love, but because the brave was the son of a sky spirit, her father had forbidden her to marry him. The cruel father tied her to a rock. Day after day she wept for her lover, until her tears washed away a part of the stone, to form the arch. One day the brave returned, rescued her, and took her to the home of his sky people.

I was just about to give an enthusiastic assent to White Hawk's plan when we saw a shadowy figure coming toward us. It was a man in the dress of White Hawk's tribe. Ignoring me, he spoke rapidly in Ottawa to White Hawk. Then, as silently as he had come, he disappeared down the bluff.

"It's the chiefs at L'Arbre Croche," White Hawk said. "There is a quarrel. I'm sorry, Mary, but I have to see Mother and then go back at once." He held my face in his hands and kissed my forehead. A moment later he was gone.

I knew it would always be like that with White Hawk. There would always be some crisis calling him away. I would be like the maiden waiting for her brave, my tears melting stone. I stood looking out at the gold path the moon made on the water. Soon White Hawk's canoe would once again be gliding away from the island and away from me.

CHAPTER

3

BEFORE THE WAR OF 1812, our island of Michilimackinac had been a simple place. There had always been celebrations on the island when the *voyageurs* and traders returned, but those affairs were wild and boisterous, requiring nothing more than a fiddle and many bottles of whiskey. They were not occasions for ladies. With the end of the war and the coming of Astor's American Fur Company, everything had changed.

The whole town was given over to Astor's endeavors. There was a boatyard where his traders' canoes were repaired, and an ironworks that manufactured tomahawk blades, kettles, traps, and other trade goods. Over it all loomed the great warehouse where the pelts brought in by the traders were sorted, graded, and baled.

Only the fort was unchanged. It stood white and gleaming at the crest of the island. The English soldiers were gone, and the American flag once more flew above us. Life at the fort had never been more lively. Lieutenant Brady, the second in command at the fort, had married a Frenchwoman from Montreal who could not let a day go by without a tea or a dance. The commander of the fort, Captain Pierce, had married Josette LaFramboise, who, like many of the wives on Michilimackinac, was part French and part Indian. Josette loved nothing better than to outdo Mme. Brady's parties. In all this the Wests were prominent.

I lacked the time and the inclination for such things at most times, but on a late June afternoon, when I was hoeing corn, Elizabeth and Emma snatched me from my work. "Madame Brady is having a party to celebrate the Fourth of July," Emma said. "You must come."

"I don't know how you stand being cooped up here with no company but a cow and pigs," Elizabeth said. "Besides, it's your patriotic duty to attend the celebration of our country's birth."

"There will be fireworks," Emma coaxed, "and there's a rumor that Madame Brady will have ices to eat. Mrs. Pierce is furious, for the *glacière* has been nearly emptied out." Emma and Elizabeth were much given to French words. The *glacière* was nothing more than an ice house.

Jacques and Little Cloud had already begged me to accompany them, but I had said no. I was about to refuse again when Elizabeth said, "Of course you will have nothing to wear, but we can let you have one of our old dresses."

"I'll think about it," I said, but I had made up my mind to give Elizabeth a surprise.

As soon as they left I dragged my trunk out into the middle of the cabin floor. I had not opened it since I had returned from my visit to Angelique in England. For a moment I paused, as though lifting the cover of the trunk would let out all the memories of England and James that I had tried to put aside. England was a different world altogether. Only Papa had known what my life there had been. Who on the island of Michilimackinac would believe I had been a guest of a duke and a duchess in their castle? Who would believe that the duke's son, James Lindsay, had made me an offer of marriage and even followed me across the Atlantic Ocean?

On hearing Papa was ill, I had rushed home. When I had last seen James, he was a member of the crew on a merchant ship, the *Otter*, which had brought me to New York. Now James was someplace in America, doing what he loved best, drawing and painting. Before we parted, he had promised that he would seek me out and ask again for my hand in marriage.

I sighed as I opened the trunk. I could not help wondering whether I had been wrong to refuse James. In England I had thought of White Hawk and of the island, unwilling to give up either. Now I was back on my beloved island, but I seldom saw White Hawk, and as much as I loved the farm, there were days when I longed for some further adventure or challenging task.

I reached into the trunk and brought out one of the ball gowns purchased for me by Mrs. Cunningham, Angelique's wealthy mother-in-law. The gown was a rich green silk, chosen for me by my sister. "It shows off your red hair, Mary," she had said, as if that had ever been my wish. The bodice of the gown was beaded, and the collar and sleeves were trimmed in lace as delicate as cobwebs. I knew there had never been such a gown on Michilimackinac. How I wished White Hawk were going to be at the ball to see me, but after coming back to the island to see Mrs. Sinclair off for Detroit on Marie and Pierre Bonnart's sloop, White Hawk had returned to L'Arbre Croche.

I held up the gown in front of me and closed my eyes, the better to recall the last time I had worn it. Around and around the cabin I glided, humming one of the waltzes that had been all the rage in London. I saw the great hall of Lindsay House lit by hundreds of candles. I recalled the duke with his stern expression and the duchess, Lady Elinor, with her kind smile. I saw James, with his blond curls that tumbled over his forehead, and his readiness to make a joke of everything.

I sensed someone else in the room and opened my eyes to find Emma standing in the doorway staring at me, her mouth agape. She fell onto a chair. "Mary! Where could you have found such a gown? I have never seen anything so handsome."

"I can't tell you, but I mean to wear it to Madame Brady's party. Only you have to promise to keep it a secret from your mother and Elizabeth." A smile crept across Emma's face. Though she was spoiled, she was only a little spoiled, and Elizabeth's rude and thoughtless ways troubled her.

"I promise. Elizabeth will be so envious." Elizabeth was ever anxious to show her superiority over her younger sister. Emma welcomed the chance to have a secret from her.

"There is one worry," I said. "In such a gown, how will I manage the rocky path through bushes and brambles to the fort?"

"You shall bring the dress down and change in my room. Mother has hired a *calèche* to carry us to the fort. Oh, Mary, how we shall enjoy the look on Elizabeth's face." Emma hugged me from sheer pleasure. "But Mary," she said, holding me at arm's length and examining my hands and face, still grubby from the hoeing. "You must promise to give yourself a good scrubbing. And one thing more. I didn't want to mention it in front of Elizabeth, for she is so fond of Mr. Brandson. Promise to be pleasant to him, and could you ask Jacques to mind his manners? It would be very sad if there were a fight at the party."

I guessed that Emma was as concerned for Jacques as she was for Mr. Brandson, and I promised to talk with my brother. "But Emma, you know Jacques. I cannot promise he will behave."

Perhaps it was my thoughts of London and the ball at Lindsay House that witched a letter to me from Angelique across the sea:

May 4, 1818
St. John's Wood
London, England

My dearest Mary,

How I wish you were here to curl up beside me so that we might have one of our long talks. How wise you were to encourage Daniel and myself to leave his parents and move into our own dear little home. I am relieved to have escaped the fuss and formality of the Cunninghams' house. Mrs. Cunningham still interferes, but now it is from a remove. Each morning notes come from her to remind me how to care for my precious Matthew. How I wish Papa had lived to see his grandson. At least our son bears Papa's name rather than the hideous Cunningham family name of Edgebolton.

You will be interested to hear that James has written to tell his parents, the duke and duchess, that he is traveling about the American wilderness, painting. He is much taken with the

Indians and the great stretches of countryside. Of course the duke and duchess wish him to return to take on the responsibilities of Castle Oakbridge and its estates, for the duke is not well. Lady Elinor speaks of you often.

Here there is rejoicing because England has added yet more of the Indian continent to its possessions. You tell me it is the same over there, where lands are taken from America's Indians. Daniel tells me it is progress, but I cannot think such seizures right and respect White Hawk for fighting against such thievery.

By the time you receive this letter, Mary, it will be summer on the island. The fragrant lilacs and the other tender spring flowers will have come and gone once more without me. There is word a steamship is to cross the Atlantic in less than a month's time. Can that be possible? I tell Daniel that one day we must take such a journey, but for now we will have to make do with letters. Write me soon and tell me of all our dear friends and of Renard and Little Cloud and Jacques (who will not put pen to paper).

All my love,
Angelique

In the week that followed, I read and reread Angelique's letter until the creases split and the writing was blotched from much handling. In my reply to Angelique I told her of the ball and the surprise I had planned for Elizabeth and Mrs. West. I made no mention of Jacques's fight with Mr. Brandson, for it would only have troubled her.

When Jacques and Little Cloud called for me on the evening of the Fourth, I remembered my promise to Emma. "You won't roll about on the floor with Mr. Brandson tonight?" I asked Jacques as we all walked down the path to town.

"Why should you think I might lose my temper with Brandson, Mary? That's all in the past. You know I'm the most gentle person in the world."

My slapdash brother was hardly recognizable in a fine coat, breeches, and silk stockings. Little Cloud wore a dress of the softest deerskin. It was a two-skin dress that draped gracefully from her shoulders. The sleeves, yoke, hem, and side seams were all fringed. The front of the dress was embroidered with beads and quills. Her thick black braids were oiled and glistening.

"What dress do you carry?" Little Cloud

asked me as we parted. In reply I only smiled and waved as I hurried toward the Wests, leaving Little Cloud and Jacques to go on to the fort.

Mrs. West frowned when she saw me with a dress wrapped in a length of muslin. "Mary, I thought you were to wear one of my girls' old dresses. I recall nothing of yours that is suitable. Elizabeth and I will go on ahead. Emma, you must stay and find something for Mary. Perhaps she could have Elizabeth's lavender dress. There is a stain where tea was spilled, but it's in the back where it won't show if Mary keeps to a chair. I'm afraid that having had no lessons and few occasions for practice, you will not be likely to dance."

Mrs. West called over her shoulder, "We will send the *calèche* back for you." She and Elizabeth hurried from the room. Their headdresses, an enormous bow in Elizabeth's hair and three curled plumes in Mrs. West's, quivered as they went.

"Now quickly, Mary." Emma took the dress from me and shook out the silken folds. I slipped it over my head and struggled into matching silk slippers with ribbons that crisscrossed over my ankles. Emma, her mouth stuck as full of hairpins as a porcupine's tail, brushed and curled and twisted my hair. Just as all the primping was making me want to escape to the woods, she pronounced me finished. Off we went in the two-wheeled carriage, with Émile swaying on the driver's seat and his elderly horse, Celestine, trotting slowly up the steep incline to the fort.

The dance was held in the fort's mess hall. Tables had been pushed back to the walls. The wooden planks of the floor were nearly white with scrubbing, though nothing could quite remove the smell of salt pork and cabbage. To soften the military hardness of the room, Mrs. Brady had placed vases of field daisies about and hung lanterns from the ceiling. During the war with England, when for three years the fort had been manned by red-coated British soldiers, Angelique had come to the fort to dances. I thought that disloyal and would not attend. Now the room was full of American soldiers dressed in their best blue uniforms, their gold buttons and braid gleaming in the lantern light. On a small platform at the end of the room, M. André and his friends were busy with their fiddles.

I took all this in as I quietly entered the hall. A moment later everyone's eyes were upon me. Looking astonished, Jacques marched over to me. “You can’t be my sister! Who are you, and where did you get that dress?”

Across the room I saw Mrs. West. Her mouth was open, and she was hanging on to Elizabeth, whose face was drained of color. They were as flustered as two hens whose eggs have been snatched from under them. Emma whispered, “Elizabeth is livid.”

The sets were just forming for a quadrille. One of the officers came up to claim me, and we began the dance with bows and curtseys all around. I had often danced the quadrille in England and fell easily into the patterns.

I never lacked for partners or for stares. As the evening went on, I was surprised to find Mr. Brandson often at my side. He waved the young officers away to claim dances for himself. When it was time for refreshments, he led me to the table, where, as promised, there were little bowls of ices among the cakes. I did not like Mr. Brandson. His hands were sweaty, and he hopped about like a rabbit. He was a rude man with manners slathered over him as frosting is piled upon a poorly baked cake to hide its faults. He could talk only of himself, of his successes with the company, and of his prospects when the company came to recognize his true worth.

I tolerated him because I wanted his forgiveness for Jacques. I knew my brother would have a hard time on the island if the fur company were against him. The company ruled the town. Yet I had to admit there was mischief in my kindness to Mr. Brandson. I could not forget the unkind remarks made by Elizabeth and Mrs. West. I was not unhappy to have the attentions of the man Elizabeth had singled out for her own.

Nothing good could come of such a motive. Jacques did not understand my purpose and spent the evening glowering at me. If Jacques was angry at my politeness to Mr. Brandson, Elizabeth was in a rage.

As the music resumed I let myself be led by Mr. Brandson onto the floor. The fiddlers swung into the quick, merry music of a polka. The room was a swirl of blue uniforms and colorful dresses. Jacques and Little Cloud spun by, and then Emma with a young officer. Emma shot a warning look at me. I paid no attention. A moment later Elizabeth and her partner were whirling beside me. I saw Elizabeth put out her foot. I felt the bite of her shoe's sharp heel and heard the sound of silk tearing. A part of my skirt ripped, revealing my petticoat. I broke away from Mr. Brandson and escaped through the door.

Jacques and Little Cloud were there in a moment. Little Cloud exclaimed over my dress. "So beautiful, green as the grass in my village. Now all spoiled."

Jacques was less kind. "It serves you right for making sheep's eyes at that miserable excuse for a man. At least when I fought Brandson I fought him out in the open, not in the way you went after Elizabeth."

I had no answer, for I knew Jacques was right. Sending my brother and Little Cloud back to the hall, I stumbled out of the fort and along the path to our farm, gathering up my skirts to cover my petticoat, sobbing as I went.

I saw how foolish I had been to let Elizabeth's insults govern me. In my behavior I was no better than she was. I kicked off my slippers, but even as I felt with relief the earth beneath my feet, still warm from the July sun, I did not see how I could ever go about again amongst my friends.

CHAPTER 4

AFTER A MISERABLE AND sleepless night I was up early to milk Belle, taking comfort in resting my cheek against her warm flank. When Belle and her calf had been led into the pasture, I turned toward the wild side of the island. To give myself an excuse for neglecting my work on the farm, I had snatched up a basket, meaning to hunt for a patch of wild raspberries. My plodding step along the narrow deer path sent chipmunks and squirrels scattering. The forest thickened, shutting me in. A covey of grouse exploded into the air with a whirr. Thorny berry branches formed a cage of briars around me. I began to pick, waiting until the bottom of my basket was covered before I allowed myself to eat one of the raspberries. The berry was so tasty, so fragrant and juicy, I felt some of my misery fall away. I picked and picked, paying no mind to the scratches on my arms and the snags on my skirt from the thorns. I made myself think of nothing but filling my basket and of the pie and preserves I would make.

It was only when I was on my way home to the farm that my foolish behavior of the night before returned to haunt me. I was sure everyone on the island would be talking of my behavior. I did not know how I would face my friends. I resolved to stay hidden on the farm.

When I returned from my lonely walk I found Jacques sitting on the doorstep in a happy frame of mind. "I'm taking my canoe over to L'Arbre Croche to see White Hawk and his people. The Indians there have some excellent corn that ripens early. I want to see if they'll give me some seed this fall. I'll only be gone two days, and

Little Cloud will see to things. She's promised to milk Belle and keep an eye on your place. Come with me, Mary. It will do us both good."

I was grateful to Jacques, for I suspected the trip was more for my benefit than his, though I knew he was ever ready for a holiday from farm work. "Yes," I said, taking my first deep breath since the party. "How soon can we leave?" I was already looking forward to seeing White Hawk.

We left the next morning in Jacques's canoe, skimming easily over the water. The lake had borrowed its color from the sky so that we could not tell whether we were on water or among the clouds. As we paddled along Jacques serenaded me with one of the ballads the traders sang to speed them on their way. As he sang a verse in French, I sang it in English. French had been our mama's language. I had learned it from my cradle, for amongst the *voyageurs* and traders on Michilimackinac French words were more common than English.

Dans un chemin j'ai rencountré
Trois chevaliers très bien montés,
Deux à cheval, l'autre à pied,
O lari li o don.

Upon the road I met one day
Three cavaliers on holiday.
Two were on horses, the other nay,
O lari li o don.

Our voices were carried out over the lake. We paddled hour after hour, finally growing silent in the long July twilight, content to watch the circling gulls. The sun fell below the horizon, painting the lake orange and our canoe and ourselves with it. At last we caught sight of the bark-covered lodges and teepees of L'Arbre Croche. When they discovered our approaching canoe, the Indians gathered along the shore, curious to see who we were. Even Jacques was silenced by the sight of so many Indians in deerskins and calicoes, hats and turbans and feathers, all made mysterious in the darkening twilight.

It was White Hawk himself who ran down to the water to greet us and pull the canoe onto the sand. "Mary! Jacques! Did you drop from the sky? There is no one I would rather see. What brings you here?"

"My sister made a great fool of herself," Jacques said. "I'm taking her away from the island for a day or two until the gossips are done with her."

At first I was hurt at Jacques's plain words, but in truth they did me good, and a minute later I was telling White Hawk the whole tale and laughing as I told it. White Hawk laughed as well. He had not a word of blame, for he saw that I had already punished myself.

"There is no ballroom here," White Hawk said, "and no occasion for silk dresses, but we can offer you a companionable fire and something to eat." Soon we were seated by a bonfire, enjoying thick corn soup flavored with maple syrup.

One of the chiefs, Black Kettle, came to greet us. White Hawk translated his words. "Welcome to our village. Friends of White Hawk are our friends. Our teepee will be your teepee tonight. It will be an honor to have you with us."

We accepted his invitation gratefully. After he left, White Hawk said, "He is one of the chiefs who is holding out against selling land here. There is another chief who cares only for the money he can get from the government. He sees the Indians from the south of the Michigan territory getting gold and trade goods each year in exchange for land they have sold. He is greedy for such things. He doesn't realize that his people's land is more precious than all the gold he can get for it. If the land goes, his people will live only at the pleasure of the government. There will be no land for hunting or for their crops."

He shrugged as if he were shifting a heavy burden. "I won't worry you with my troubles. Come and meet some of my people."

Up and down the beach the campfires made friendly circles of light. Children and dogs played at the edges of the circles. People were dancing, and some sat around the fires telling stories. White Hawk translated an argument between two men. One insisted a bow and arrow was better than a gun. "You might be sure of gaining your target with a gun, but its loud sound will frighten away other animals."

"But in a war," the second man argued, "it will be the enemy who will be frightened away."

The first man began to tell tales of his bravery in past wars, while the other, much to Jacques's delight, told tales of his great hunting deeds.

At another fire there was grumbling. One of the men spoke English, and I heard him say to Jacques and White Hawk, "It has happened again. It is devils that appear by night. How are we to protect our sacred burial grounds from such spirits?"

"They are not spirits," White Hawk said. "They are grave robbers."

"Can't you catch them?" Jacques asked.

"They come in the dark of night," White Hawk said. "We never know when. But it's nothing for you to worry about. After all your paddling you must be tired. Let me show you to Black Kettle's teepee. Many people sleep there, so it's important to respect people's privacy. Keep your eyes down when you enter, and settle where you are told. And, Jacques, you are not to chatter to those sleeping next to you. You must imagine there are invisible walls around the others."

As we entered the teepee I could smell the fragrance of the fresh cedar boughs scattered on the ground and the pungent smoke from a dying fire. There were baskets of corn and potatoes, piles of firewood and birch bark dishes. A few clothes were hung from nails pounded into the ridgepole. I kept my eyes down and tiptoed around the chief and his wife, who were already asleep on a bed of bearskins. Farther around the circle were whom I took to be his son and the son's wife and then two small children asleep with their arms flung around one another. We saw an empty space where some deerskins had been spread out. I settled down, but Jacques, after a hasty look around, whispered, "I'll sleep under the stars. All this is too sociable for me."

And sociable it was—and cozy. At first I was kept awake by the closeness of the other sleepers and their stirrings and murmurings, but soon, with the example of sleep all about me, I drifted off, waking only once when I heard an owl hoot nearby.

In the morning Jacques went to investigate the cornfields while White Hawk and I wandered along the edge of the lake. Women were already gathering fish from nets that had been set out on poles the night before. They were plucking out the slippery fish and throwing them into baskets. The fish would be scaled and cleaned and put to dry on the wooden racks that stood nearby. The smell of drying fish was everywhere. White Hawk said, "One gill net is worth many acres of farmland, but you can't get through a northern Michigan winter with just dried fish, and the corn crop is doing poorly this year."

As we passed them, a few of the women gave me a curious look. I knew that in their eyes White Hawk was an eligible man, but no matter how much they might admire him, none of the unmarried Indian women would have done something so immodest as to walk alone with him.

When we were out of sight of the women, White Hawk took off his moccasins and I unlaced my boots, the better to enjoy the warmth of the sand and the lick of the small waves as they came in and cooled our toes. The lake was painted with stripes of dark blue, green, and turquoise. Two loons were bobbing near shore. From time to time they would push up out of the water and beat their wings in some loon splashing game. A small procession of wagging sandpipers ran ahead of us, tossing up snail shells and probing the sand in their hunger for insects. White Hawk reached down to pick up a gull feather and tucked it into my hair. "There. Now you're a proper Indian maiden."

We were alone on the beach that stretched as far as the eye could see. "If we walked enough miles south along this beach we would come to Fort Dearborn," I said. "From there we could go north along the sands to Green Bay and from there to Saint Ignace, and that is only a short canoe trip from Michilimackinac. A circle of empty beach."

"I'm afraid those beaches won't be empty for long," White Hawk answered in a troubled voice. "I heard talk in Detroit of the building of a canal connecting the Hudson River with Lake

Erie. Such a canal will bring more settlers looking for land."

We flung ourselves down at the water's edge. I began to scoop up the damp sand. Long ago, when we were only children, White Hawk and I had built sand villages with houses and forts. Now I started a castle. White Hawk playfully joined me. His worried look had disappeared.

"There should be a moat here," I said. "And a drawbridge. And there must be lots of chimneys sticking up like this, for every room has its own fireplace. Over here we must make a stable and a coach house." I scooped up more sand. I put towers on my castle and marked out windows and massive doors. When I finished I realized I had made a small Castle Oakbridge.

White Hawk was studying me. "This castle is not something you imagined. Your hands are following some picture in your mind. Is it possible you know such a place? Is it the place where you wore that costume you spoke of?"

"I do know such a place, and such dresses are worn there every night for dinner."

White Hawk looked glum. "Our dinner last night must have seemed a poor thing."

I put my hand on his arm and smiled up at him. "It was better than all the fancy dinners I had at Oakbridge put together. Just imagine swallowing with a footman behind your chair staring down at every bite you take. Imagine rows of strange forks and knives and spoons to puzzle you. And all the while you must keep up a polite conversation and resist loosening the waist of your dress, which is crushing you, or kicking off your shoes, which are pinching your toes."

White Hawk laughed. "I wish I had been there to see you on your good behavior. Tell me what were you doing at such a place. Angelique and Daniel surely don't live in a castle."

I hesitated. I had always told White Hawk the truth. In a small voice I admitted, "There was a young man, James Lindsay."

"This young man, this James Lindsay, was attached to you?"

I nodded.

"And were you attached to him?"

"I left England to return to the island." This time the truth in my answer was as slippery as the fish we had seen earlier.

White Hawk knew it. "That is no answer, Mary. You left to return to your father. What of this James Lindsay? Could a man in such a position have serious intentions toward you?"

In a small voice I said, "Yes, he did, and strange as it may seem, his mother, Lady Elinor, and his father, the duke, wished it as well. James would not take responsibility for Oakbridge. His parents believed a marriage would make him settle down."

"And what did you think, Mary? Did you want to marry him?" White Hawk held my face gently between his hands so that I could not look away.

I could not lie to White Hawk. In a faltering voice I said, "I did think about it." I wanted to tell White Hawk that my refusing James had as much to do with my feelings for him as it had to do with my wish to hurry home to Papa, but White Hawk sprang up and began walking back toward the village. I had to run to keep up with him. I would have given much to take my words back, but there was no magic way to do that.

I touched his arm. "Please believe me, White Hawk. Nothing could make me happier than being back on the island with all the people I love."

At those words White Hawk slowed a bit. His face relaxed into a smile. He said, "And those who love you, Mary." He linked his arm in mine. We walked silently back to the camp.

We found a disappointed Jacques in the village. "The cornfields are parched from lack of rain. The crop will be meager this year, and what little corn there is will have to be sold to the soldiers at the fort and to Astor. The Indians need the money."

"It's not just the money," White Hawk said. "If they don't send the corn, Astor and the Fort will soon find it elsewhere, and L'Arbre Croche will lose its market. I'm afraid there will be hunger here when winter comes."

As we were talking a young man ran toward us, an angry look on his face. The man spoke to White Hawk. Because he had been a trader, Jacques understood many of the Algonquin languages, including that of the Ottawa. Now he translated the man's words for me. "One of this tribe's graves has been robbed. Two white men loitering around the village are suspected."

White Hawk said, "We had heard of grave robbers desecrating the graves of other tribes. We did not think it would happen here. Now it has happened not once but twice."

Horrified, I asked, "Why would they dig up a grave?"

White Hawk said, "It's our custom to bury possessions with the body of the dead person, silver ornaments and richly embroidered clothing. This is especially true for a chief." White Hawk's voice was hard. "I can think of no crime more terrible than dishonoring our sacred burial grounds."

"Isn't there some way we could catch them?" I asked.

"I'll find the men and shoot them," Jacques shouted. Since neither White Hawk nor I believed Jacques meant what he said, we paid him no attention.

In a small voice I suggested, "We could have a funeral for a chief and then watch his grave."

"Which of our chiefs would you kill?" White Hawk asked in a voice full of irony.

"I'm serious."

"So am I. Our chiefs are anxious to catch the men, but not so anxious as to give up their lives."

"Don't tease me, White Hawk. Why couldn't we just *say* that a chief has died and make a big show of it so the robbers would know? You have said they lurk about the village. When they came to rob the grave, we would catch them."

"What if they didn't come right away?" Jacques asked.

"If you plan to open a grave," White Hawk pointed out, "the sooner you do it, the better."

He gave me a thoughtful look. “Let me talk to the chiefs.”

The robbing of the sacred burial grounds so angered the chiefs that they agreed to this odd plan. Chief Black Kettle was selected, and he went into hiding as his people prepared for an elaborate funeral.

Relatives of the chief put on their oldest clothes and painted large black circles around their eyes. They put all their energy into the sham funeral. There was a great shrieking and wailing by the members of the tribe. A constant drumbeat was kept up. The commotion would surely be heard by anyone within miles of the village.

While the chief hid in a nearby teepee, the members of the tribe rose one by one to tell stories of his fine character and courage. White Hawk said the chief was pleased to hear so many kind things about himself and was getting quite puffed up.

A bundle of rags was arranged in the shape of a man’s body. It was wrapped in birch bark and tied up with basswood cord. The next morning, with much moaning and wailing, the “chief” was carried to the graveyard and placed in a shallow grave with his pipe, tobacco pouch, and silver jewelry. They were so pleased with their performances, the wailing people were reluctant to put an end to it.

That night, White Hawk and Jacques and two members of the tribe prepared to hide themselves in the woods near the graveyard to wait. I begged to go with them, but White Hawk forbade it. "There is sure to be some sort of fight."

"That's unfair. It was my idea."

"If we catch them," White Hawk said, "I have a plan of my own, and you shall play an important role in it." With that I had to be satisfied.

It was daylight when White Hawk and the others returned. No one had appeared in the graveyard, though Jacques had thought he had seen movement in the woods. He had wanted to go after whoever it was, but White Hawk insisted the men must be caught in the act.

The next night they set off again, this time with less hope. Clouds moved across the moon and drifted away again. I could imagine the graveyard under the light of the moon and then in darkness. I was almost glad I wasn't there. The whole village kept vigil. At midnight we were still sitting around the campfires. Children, as always allowed to stay up as late as they pleased, were curled up on blankets or asleep on their mothers' laps. One little boy, too restless to sleep, wandered away from his campfire toward the edge of the woods. Suddenly he called out.

A moment later White Hawk and Jacques and the other watchers appeared, dragging two struggling white men. The first man had a turkey look to him with his small head, large chest, short legs, and indignant squawking. The other man was silent, but he appeared the more dangerous of the two. He was thin, with sharp hatchetlike features and narrowed shifty eyes.

A great shout went up from those of us around the campfire. I wondered what would be done to the thieves now that they had been captured. There was no white man's court or even an officer of the law for miles around. I watched with increasing worry as two poles were sunk firmly into the ground. The two men, both their faces now white with fear, were dragged struggling to the poles and bound.

One by one the members of the tribes went up to examine the hair of their captives, holding it up and smiling in anticipation. One by one they returned to their seats around the campfire and began sharpening their scalping knives. The two men cried out for mercy, but no one paid them attention.

At last White Hawk faced the men. Pretending he knew only a few words of English, he said, "Bad medicine to kill at night. Morning, first thing, we scalp. Put to death." He appeared to have remembered something and added, "After much torture. Now we sleep so we are strong in morning."

With that the Indians all entered their teepees. I followed White Hawk into Black Kettle's teepee. Their performance had been so impressive I half believed them and was about to plead for the lives of the men when I saw that everyone was trying to keep their laughter from carrying outside the teepee.

White Hawk whispered, "Now you'll have your fun, Mary. Wait an hour and then take this knife out with you. Tell the men that since you are a white girl you feel sorry for them and you'll cut their cords and allow them to escape. But first tell them they must promise never to be found anywhere around here and never to raid another Indian grave."

Jacques was grinning. "It's all right if you want to poke them a little with the knife, like you do to a roast goose."

I was excited to be playing a part in the plan and waited impatiently for the hour to pass. When White Hawk signaled that it was time, I picked up White Hawk's knife and stole softly outside. The two men were whining and mumbling to each other, blaming one another for what had happened to them. When they saw me with a knife in my hand, the turkey man groaned, but the other one said, "She's a white girl. She's not going to scalp us."

I looked hastily back at the teepee, pretending I was afraid of being seen. I whispered the words White Hawk had told me to say. Hatchet Face was quick to assure me, "We'll never rob another grave so long as we live." Turkey Man said, "We'll never go anywhere near a graveyard, even when we're dead."

As soon as I cut the cords of the hatchet-faced man he grabbed the knife from my hand and freed Turkey Man, who quickly began to run toward the forest. For a moment Hatchet Face stood looking at me. "There's something strange here," he said. He was about to reach out for me when White Hawk and the other Indians shot out of the teepee yelling, their tomahawks raised. In a second both men had disappeared into the woods.

Afterward Chief Black Kettle thanked me. White Hawk translated the chief's words for me. "Your plan was a good one. Good for me, too. It was the best funeral I will ever have, for I heard many nice things about me. At my next funeral I think I will not be able to hear so much."

The next morning, as White Hawk was helping to push our canoe off the beach, he promised he would soon be on the island. Then he whispered to me, "If it's a castle you want, Mary, I'll build you one of logs. You can wear your fine dress to dinner and ease your waist and take off your shoes whenever you wish."

CHAPTER 5

IT WAS THE END of July. The cabbages were beginning to form pale green heads. I had picked my first mess of beans. In the woods the nesting birds had quieted. White Hawk had returned and was staying down in the Indian camp trying to pick up information from some Ojibwas who had just returned from Detroit. There had been time for only one afternoon's ramble in the woods and a hasty visit to the eagle's nest. Though I longed for more time with White Hawk, the farm claimed all of my attention. Potato bugs multiplied faster than I could pick them off the plants. Weeds sprang up in the cornfield. On a day when the sun beat so hotly on the ground I could not walk barefoot, I was standing by the fireplace stirring a boiling kettle of gooseberries. I thought it a terrible injustice that gooseberries would ripen in the hottest month of the year instead of in the winter, when a fire and a boiling kettle would be welcome. I was wearing my oldest dress, for the preserves spattered as they cooked. Every now and then a drop of perspiration fell from the end of my nose into the kettle. I tried to cheer myself by thinking of how White Hawk had promised to come in the afternoon to take me for a swim in the cool waters of the lake.

I looked up to see a stranger standing at the open door of the cabin, a pack on his back and a leather case under his arm. He was tall and thin with long tangled yellow curls and a curly yellow beard that all but hid his face. "Ah, I see now, Mary, why you ran away from me. You wanted the comforts, ease, and elegance of your present life."

"James!" I knew the voice at once, recognizing the waggish tone. With James nothing could be serious. I ran to greet him, and then ran back to stir the kettle, for the gooseberries were about to boil over. "How did you come here? How did you find me?"

"I've been on your island since yesterday trying to discover where to find you. I spent last night in a boardinghouse. I've been drawing portraits of the Indians and getting up the courage to see you. You won't send me away?"

"How can you say such a thing! Of course you won't be sent away. I am delighted. I want to show you the island, and my brother and sister-in-law and all of our friends must meet you."

"Have I come all the way across the ocean to be exhibited like some curious creature? Am I to have no time with you, Mary?"

Hastily I pushed some crocks at him. "Hold these, James, while I ladle out the preserves from the kettle. It must be now, or the gooseberries won't set. No, no. Like this." I laughed, for James was ever incapable of a practical task.

When the kettle was empty, I pulled James over to the table and poured him some cider. As I sat across from him I rejoiced in the good nature and fun that shone from his blue eyes. "Let me see your drawings, James," I begged. James was a fine artist, and all the ridicule that came so easily to his tongue disappeared when he held pencil or quill in his hand.

He opened his case. One by one he handed me drawings, telling me of the travels that had taken him to each place. There were sketches of wide rivers with barges and sailboats and of narrow streams flowing through tangles of trees and brush. There was a drawing of a doe with two speckled fawns and many of Indian villages with their hundreds of teepees. Because James was ever fond of putting people down on paper, "capturing their soul," as he called it, there were many pictures of Indian men and women.

"This drawing of an Indian was done only last night," he said. "I was at some distance from the young man, watching him talk with two Indians who appeared to be chiefs. I thought him a fine figure of a noble savage."

I looked at the picture. It was White Hawk. "Savage" indeed! I was about to enlighten James when White Hawk himself walked through the door. The two men looked at one another. White Hawk could have no idea that this disheveled traveler was the resident of Castle Oakbridge, and James knew nothing of White Hawk but his outward appearance. I hardly knew how to begin.

James spoke first. "Here is the very Indian I sketched! I hope, sir, you have no objection to my little picture." He held it out for White Hawk to see.

As he studied the drawing, a half vexed, half amused look came over White Hawk's face. The amused part won, and White Hawk smiled at James.

James mistook White Hawk's silence. "I see he has no English," James said. "I wonder if it might not be a useful venture to instruct him in a few English words, for in my experience the Indians are ready learners."

I gave White Hawk a quick look. Choking down my laughter I said, "I'm afraid only a few English words would not do for him."

"A pity. I would like to get to know him better." James sighed. "I must admit that although I've traveled much through Indian country, I have learned little of the Indians' languages."

"'*Non omnia possumus omnes,*'" White Hawk said.

A puzzled look appeared on James's face. "What a strange language your Indian speaks. If I didn't know better I would have thought that was Latin, though I would be the last to recognize a Latin word. I'm afraid it is a language I never had the brains to master."

White Hawk said, "Then let me translate the

words of the Latin poet Virgil for you. Perhaps you'll agree they are fitting: '*Non omnia possumus omnes.*' 'We are not all capable of everything.'"

The parts of James's face that were not bearded turned a deep red. He sprang out of his chair. In an angry voice he said, "The two of you have made a fool of me!"

"I think, sir," White Hawk said, "you give us too much credit. There were more than two at work on the task. Surely some of the credit belongs to you."

I had never known James's good nature to fail him, and it did not fail him now. He began to laugh and could hardly stop. White Hawk and I joined in. Finally James managed to say, "I knew there was fighting in this country between the white man and the Indian. I did not know the Indians won their wars by hurling Latin words at a fellow. Give me arrows anytime." He put out his hand. "James Lindsay, sir. May I have the honor of knowing the name of the man who has properly thrashed me without laying a hand on me?"

White Hawk's whole body stiffened. I could see that he recognized James as the Lord Lindsay who was attached to me. "I am White Hawk," he said in a cold voice, "or perhaps you would be more comfortable calling me Gavin Sinclair."

Gavin was the name the Sinclairs had given White Hawk.

James was at once sensible of the change in White Hawk. He too became serious. "I see that I have offended you, sir, and I most humbly beg your pardon."

The two men stood there, neither one uttering a word. I was miserable. There was nothing I wished for more than to have these two men, both so dear to me, become friends. What would have happened had Jacques not burst through the door I can't tell. Jacques looked from one to the other and said, "White Hawk, why are you glowering at this stranger? And why is he glowering back?" To James he said, "I'm Jacques O'Shea, Mary's brother. Who are you?"

"This is James Lindsay," I said, "who has come all the way from England and who was so kind to me when I was visiting Angelique." For fear of how he would have ragged me, I had never told Jacques about my visits to Castle Oakbridge or James's attentions to me.

Jacques clapped James on the back. "We're happy to have the chance to repay your kindness, Mr. Lindsay. You're welcome to stay with Little Cloud and me. Mary, let's have a gathering for James tomorrow so that our friends may meet him. You'll come, White Hawk?"

White Hawk had been looking from me to James and back again. Now he replied, "I'm afraid I have to return to L'Arbre Croche tomorrow." He made a stiff bow to James. "I hope I have the pleasure of seeing you again, sir. Will you be long on the island?"

James grinned at me and to my great embarrassment said, "I will stay on the island as long as Mary will put up with me. I am hoping that before I leave I can induce Mary to make another trip to London."

At this, White Hawk looked as angry as a bear. With a formal good-bye, he turned to leave. I longed to run after him and tell him that I had nothing to do with James's appearance and certainly nothing to do with his plans for me. With James and Jacques there, I could do nothing of the kind. I had to watch helplessly as White Hawk walked away.

Jacques asked James to tell him about his travels. James had made his way up the great Mississippi to Prairie du Chien and along the Fox River to Green Bay.

"Why, that's my old route," Jacques exclaimed. "You must tell me how it is now."

White Hawk's behavior was soon forgotten

by the two men as they tried to outdo one another in tales of outlandish adventure. There was much talk of the Sioux and bragging about escapes from their tomahawks and scalping knives. The stories were told as boasts, and no one among the three of us believed a word.

Once I had very nearly agreed to marrying James. I would have been mistress of a grand castle with miles of farmland and all the sheep and hogs I could wish for. When Papa became ill I had hurried away, leaving James and returning to the island and to White Hawk, who was ever on my mind. Now James had reappeared, and White Hawk had heard him say he meant to carry me back to England. I did not know how I was ever to sort things out.

The next evening our friends came to meet James, who had settled in quite happily with Jacques and Little Cloud. Only White Hawk was absent. With no further word for me, he had returned that day to L'Arbre Croche.

James and Jacques had gone out with their guns in the morning, returning with enough grouse for a pie. I believe Jacques thought James had learned his shooting on some wild stretch of woodland as he had. He did not guess that at

James's home, Castle Oakbridge, grouse were flushed from the grasses by twenty hired beaters so that the owners and their guests might have the pleasure of murdering them.

Into the pie went new potatoes, onions, and little carrots, all freshly dug. I seasoned the stew with rosemary and thyme from my herb garden. Little Cloud brought a birch bark basket full of wild blackberries, and Belle furnished the milk from which I took thick cream to go over them. The MacNeils arrived with a bottle of wine made from the grapes that Angus MacNeil tended when he was not at his blacksmith's forge. "You will not have tasted the likes of this in England," he said to James, making me think of the clusters of crystal wineglasses upon the table at Oakbridge.

Pere Mercier greeted James warmly. "Church of England, I suppose, sir, and your Sunday morning, spent in some great stone cathedral. Still, you are welcome to worship with us at our humble little church."

The Wests were the last to arrive. I could see the promise of a guest from London had caused them to take pains with their dress. Mrs. West was in her best black silk, her pearl brooch at her neck. Emma wore her shawl. Elizabeth had a new bonnet shaped like a dented kettle with so many feathers to it that, had she wished, she could surely have taken flight.

Mrs. West and her daughters looked about for an English gentleman. "Your visitor has not arrived as yet?" Mrs. West asked.

"Oh, yes," I replied, leading James over to them. They stared at James's untrimmed hair and bushy beard, at his rough clothes and worn boots. "This is James Lindsay," I said.

Dr. West shook his hand warmly, but Mrs. West and Elizabeth gave him only a cold acknowledgment. After a quick greeting, Emma's attention was diverted by some of James's sketches, which I had set about. Though she was modest about her efforts, Emma took great pleasure in painting pretty pictures of flowers. "Oh, Mary, who did these excellent drawings? I have never seen better."

"They are James's work," I told her.

Emma turned her large brown eyes upon James. "Sir, there is much in your work to admire."

Mrs. West sniffed. "The pictures are not without their good points, but could you not have found better subjects than the rough countryside?"

"I am such a ruffian, mam, I thought the subject suited me."

"Mother, look here." Emma held up the drawing of White Hawk. "It's Gavin Sinclair." Emma admired the sketch. "You have captured him to the life, hasn't he, Papa?"

"Indeed." Dr. West held the paper far away from his eyes so that he could make it out.

James laughed. "Now that I have met him, I would make another drawing all together." Then James told the story of how White Hawk had made sport of him. He told the story in such a droll way and with such good humor that everyone laughed, and soon we were sitting about the table, talking most pleasantly.

Dr. West wished to hear what James knew about the advances of medicine in England. Pere Mercier said he was glad Catholics were no longer murdered there. Emma spoke of how she longed to see the paintings in the great castles. Elizabeth said she had heard women went about inside their houses wearing turbans like Indians. Mrs. MacNeil wanted to know if it was true that in England cheeses were eaten after the dessert. Her husband wanted to hear about the new Waterloo Bridge that crossed the Thames. "Of the most intricate construction I hear, sir."

All these questions James answered with the greatest patience and courtesy. No word was spoken of Lindsay House, his elegant home in London, or of the fine paintings in Castle Oakbridge. He seemed to delight in his new friends. Only Mrs. West held out against his charm, whispering to me, "I wonder, Mary, that Angelique would have let you become friends with a common traveling painter."

The grouse pie was a great success, and Pere Mercier had two bowls of blackberries. Mrs. West ate with great relish, although, unlike her own fine porcelain, our china plates were thick and scalloped with chipping.

When the dinner was over Jacques and James lighted torches and escorted the guests to their homes in the village. Little Cloud and I tidied the dishes. She was as fond of being out of the house as I was, so after our efforts we sat on the doorstep, Red Fox asleep in Little Cloud's arms, waiting for Jacques and James to return. It was the last day of July. Everything was soft outside, the air so temperate it was like a second skin. We could hear the water gurgling in the nearby spring and smell the mint that grew at its edge. Even at this late hour the darkness held back. In the west a row of tall pines was sharply outlined against a fading yellow glow. A beetle beat against the lighted window. Some night animal, a raccoon or a porcupine, was thieving in the gooseberry bushes. We heard a whippoorwill call in the distance.

"That bird calls to us on the prairie," Little Cloud said. "We wait to hear it in the spring and are saddened when the cold comes and the bird leaves us."

"Do you miss your village?" I asked.

"I miss my family and my friends. Here when people come together you must start your friendship each time from the beginning. In my village friendship is like the wild grapevines that grow and grow so that you cannot find the beginning or the end. I hope someday we can take Red Fox to see my home."

After a long minute she said, "From the way he looks at you, Mary, I believe James thinks very well of you."

"I hope so. We were good friends in England."

"His looking at you is more than looking at a friend, I think."

I had longed to share my perplexities. "You mustn't tell anyone, even Jacques, but when I was in England, James asked me to marry him."

"And will you?"

"I don't know, Little Cloud. I would have to live in England. When I was there I missed the island as you miss your village. I longed to be back here."

"Was it just the island, Mary? Was there nothing else you longed for?"

I was relieved to open my heart to someone and there could be no one more trustworthy than Little Cloud. "I longed to see White Hawk again," I said. "But I don't think such longing does any good. He has always some higher purpose than me."

"Mary, I know you. I believe you could not love a man unless he had some high purpose to his life."

I knew that Little Cloud was right. Yet something troubled me. "Why must it be that only men have a high purpose, Little Cloud? Sometimes I look about the island and wish there were something I might do, something to make life here better, something beside slopping hogs and milking Belle."

Though Little Cloud's words stayed with me, there was no further talk that night of high purpose, for James and Jacques were having a race up the bluff. Jostling and tripping one another and making much use of elbows, they landed in a merry heap at our feet.

CHAPTER 6

IT WAS TEN O'CLOCK the next morning when James appeared, sleepy-eyed, at my doorway. I had been up since six so that I could bring water from the spring and heat it in the cool morning hours to do the laundry. It would be torture to have a fire going in the fireplace on a hot August afternoon. Sheets, tablecloths, and petticoats had long since been scrubbed and spread on the grass to bleach and dry.

"From a distance it looks like snow in

August," James said, admiring my display of white linen. He grinned at me. "You smell like a tub of soapsuds, Mary. And let me wipe away the ashes from your forehead. Why must you work so hard? There is no need for that. I heard that there will soon be a schooner leaving the island for Detroit. Pere Mercier could marry us, and in a few months' time we would be at Oakbridge where you would have as many washerwomen as you like."

"James, I can't leave the farm. What would happen to Belle and the chickens and pigs?"

"I'll hire the whole schooner, Mary. We'll take them along. Each pig and chicken shall have its own cabin. At Oakbridge, Belle shall sleep in the Queen's bedroom if you like."

"James, be serious," I pleaded.

Serious at last, James said, "Father isn't well, Mary." He sighed. "I'm afraid the day will come when I must return to Oakbridge, perhaps forever. When the day comes, Mary, I want to take you with me. If you aren't ready to come now, then I must learn to be a farmer so that I am of some use to you while I try to change your mind. I mean to start this minute. Tell me what is to be done."

Then began a month of such muddle and

confusion, such disaster and ruin that it was a miracle that the farm was left standing at all.

"Take Belle and her calf to the pasture," I said on this first day. Off James went, holding Belle's halter and singing to her at the top of his voice while the calf trailed along behind him, hesitating at the strange music. In an hour he was back at the door, an embarrassed look on his face. "When I reached the pasture," he said, "I saw an apple tree whose branches made a handsome pattern. I got out my pencil and sketchbook. I'm afraid I gave no thought to Belle while I sketched. Unfortunately I seem to have left the pasture gate open. It seems Belle and her child have disappeared." Off we ran, hunting the cow and calf halfway around the island.

When James brought pails of water from the spring, the little rivulet that wound toward the spring was so pretty he drew it not once but many times. When I looked into the pails that he finally brought into the cabin, I found a frog and many drowned flies.

One day, after he had offered to gather eggs, he came back from the hen coop looking distressed.

"Where are the eggs, James?" I asked.

"They were in my cap," he answered.

"And where are they now?"

"To answer that question I must turn around."

He had indeed gathered the eggs in his cap. He put down his cap to get out his sketchbook, for the hens on their nests made a fine picture. When he sat down to make the drawing, he sat on the eggs.

It was no surprise to me that James should be a clumsy farmer, for his father had grieved over his indifference to their estate. I could not be severe with James, for no one had a better nature or was more willing to try. All the little misfortunes ended in such merry laughter that they hardly seemed to matter.

If James was not a clever farmer, he was ever good company. With White Hawk gone, I found myself enjoying James's companionship. At the end of the day, when work on the farm was finished, we had long talks about the memories of England we shared. When the weather was pleasant I stole time from my tasks to show James those places on the island that I knew would call out to his painter's heart. I sat beside him while he captured the majesty of a giant pine tree or the promise of a schooner sailing into the harbor. It did not matter that James was a clumsy farmer, for he was surely a gifted artist.

I was not the only one to admire James's talent. Emma stopped by one afternoon carrying a sketchbook and paintbox. She turned her great brown eyes on James and in her soft voice said, "I have found a field where the wild asters bloom in such profusion that it looks like a purple sea. I thought Mr. Lindsay might enjoy such a sight. I'm going there to try to paint it. Perhaps he would like to accompany me."

James was ready to give an eager assent but stopped himself. "That is a good idea, but I meant to help Mary to scythe the hay field."

The thought of a sharp scythe in James's hands was terrible to me. We would be lucky to end up with our heads. "That's very kind of you, James, but it's only a very small field, and mowing is hardly an hour's work. No, no, don't think of it. You must see the island's wild asters. There is nothing like them." Hastily I pushed his sketchbook into his hands. The presence of the sketchbook reassured him, and he followed Emma out of the cabin with a light step as if he were a schoolboy let out of class.

I took up the scythe and walked out to the field. In the August afternoon grasshoppers danced around me. In the distance I could see the blue-green water that flowed around the island. The fishermen's boats bobbed like ducks on the lake. Overhead, clouds in the shape of mares' tails told me rain was coming. I would have to get the hay into the barn by evening. I grasped the two pegs on the scythe's handle and swung from right to left, making a semicircle as Papa had taught me to do. The new-mown hay smelled like summer itself. When the pocket-sized field was cleared, I got out the wooden rake and began to stack the hay, but the warmth of the afternoon and the hours of work I had done that day had made me sleepy. I dropped the rake and slumped down in the shade of an oak tree. I thought I would rest for only a few minutes, and in no time I was asleep.

When I awoke I saw that the hay had miraculously gathered itself together into three neat stacks, ready to be pitched into a cart and taken to the barn. I blinked, trying to think whether I had done the work before drifting off to sleep, or perhaps in my sleep, yet I knew I had not. James could not have done the work, or the stacks would not be so neatly made. I looked about. White Hawk rose up from behind one of the stacks.

Happy to see White Hawk, I called out,

"You've done my work for me."

"I used to mow and stack hay for my mother and father. I haven't forgotten how."

White Hawk settled down next to me, and we leaned companionably together against the tree. "What do you hear of your mother?" I asked.

"I had a letter from Mother the other day. She's happy in Detroit. I'll see her on my next visit there, but that won't be for a while. I plan to spend more time on the island." He gave me a sly grin. "I'm going to be a warrior and fight the battle of my life."

Startled, I asked, "What can you mean? There are no Indian wars on the island."

"I've returned to do battle with your James Lindsay. I was a coward to run away. I mean to cross swords with him."

Alarmed I sprung up. "He's not *my* James Lindsay, and I want nothing to do with battles. Would you have me be some medieval maiden with knights fighting over her like two dogs over a bone? Am I to have no say in this?"

White Hawk was at my side, reaching for my hands. "I've put it badly, Mary. I only mean to say I went away because I was afraid I had very little to offer you in the way of fine clothes and castles. Yet as I thought about it, I saw I was not being fair to you. I don't believe clothes and castles are what you really care for. I came back to take my chance against Lindsay."

As we stood there with my hands in White Hawk's, my face lifted to his, James and Emma appeared, hurrying along the path. When they saw us, they stopped and stared, waiting. Quickly I pulled away from White Hawk, but he did not move. White Hawk and James exchanged glances. No word was spoken, but I saw that indeed there was to be a battle. I resolved to be no medieval maiden. I would not be the spoil of some war. I would make up my own mind.

Emma always had great delicacy. Now, to cover the awkwardness, she hurried toward us and thrust her sketchbook at me. "Mary, just look at this field of wild asters. Didn't I capture the shade of purple? It is all James's doing. He told me exactly how much red and blue to mix, with just a touch of white. You must see what he has drawn. He has that little copse of birch trees to the life. Do show them, James."

James smiled, but it was not a happy smile. "Mary and Mr. Sinclair can't be interested in the little copse of birch trees."

"Of course we are. And you mustn't call White Hawk 'Mr. Sinclair.' I was just thanking him for stacking the hay for me."

James raised his eyebrows in a most irritating way. "When you sent me off, I thought the mowing was a task that you wished to do alone. Had I known such expert help was on its way, I would have gone off with a less guilty conscience."

In a gruff voice White Hawk said, "Mary had no way of knowing I would help her. I just happened by. However, I was raised on a farm, and I look forward to using whatever skill I have. I mean to assist her whenever possible."

"I am sure she will be grateful for such skilled aid," James said in a lofty voice. "I am afraid I have no talent for being of help on a farm."

"Nonsense," I said. "Just wait." I ran to the barn and got the cart. When it was empty I could pull it easily over the path to the hay field. "Now," I said, handing each man a pitchfork, "let us all get to work."

James worked very hard, but White Hawk had pitched hay all of his life. At last James threw down his pitchfork, disgusted. "I must defer to you, sir," he said. "But only in this."

He was about to walk off when I called out, "James, I have a farm task I know you will do as well as White Hawk." I pointed to the cart, heavy now with hay. "It has to be pulled to the barn. Let White Hawk take one handle and you take the other." I could not resist adding, "Let us see if the two of you can pull together."

At first I got angry looks from James and White Hawk, but a moment later they were laughing. "You have managed to make horses of us, Mary," White Hawk said.

"No," James corrected him. "She has made asses of us."

Emma and I followed along behind the cart, joining in the laughter.

Once the hay was in the barn we splashed our warm faces and hands with the water from the spring and drank cupfuls of the icy water. James spoke of returning to Jacques's farm. White Hawk said he was going to meet someone in the town, but neither of them would be the first to start off and leave me with the other. Finally they rose together and, with a careful watch on one another, to be sure the other did not return, they went their separate ways.

Emma kept her eye on James as he made his way down the path. "James has fine manners for an itinerant artist," Emma said. "Perhaps in doing portraits in England he has been exposed to people of a better class."

"I can't think what you mean by 'a better

class,' Emma. People in England are just as they are here. There are good people and bad."

"I am sure you are right, Mary. Only Mama has strong ideas as to whom we ought to associate with. Perhaps it would be better if she didn't know I had spent the afternoon with James."

I smiled to myself as I thought what Mrs. West would say if she knew the itinerant artist was Lord Lindsay of Castle Oakbridge.

White Hawk was as good as his word. He was daily at the farm. He would put his hand to any task. "The chickens are bothered with lice," I complained one day. "They are so restless with itching they will not sit still on their nests long enough to lay."

"Then we must get rid of the lice," White Hawk said, "and I know how."

While I turned the chickens out of the coop and emptied their nests of the old straw that crawled with lice, White Hawk gathered cedar boughs. We made a small fire in the coop and then sprinkled water on the smoldering boughs so that the coop was filled with fragrant smoke, pleasant to smell but hateful to lice. As we filled the nesting boxes with fresh straw, I would not have traded the sweet-smelling chicken coop for any castle.

James and White Hawk played a kind of *cache-cache*, the French game of hide-and-seek. When James knew that White Hawk was helping me on the farm, James would wander off to the Indian village to sketch, or he and Emma would ramble about looking for some picturesque scene. No sooner would White Hawk leave to visit Pere Mercier or to see to business he had with the Indians, than James would appear to lure me from my work with letters that had come from England. Often he would talk of what our life might be like—traveling where we wished or settling down at Oakbridge. It was talk of the traveling that made his face light up.

Just as James and White Hawk kept changing places, so my feeling for them changed as well. James was so cheerful a companion and so full of amusement, our time together always ended in laughter. White Hawk was more serious, but together we shared a love for our island, and every walk took us over familiar ground where we had wandered together as children.

There was something else as well. I could not help but see how the Indians on the island depended on White Hawk's counsel. I admired this in White Hawk, yet I knew that such demands might forever take him away from the island.

CHAPTER 7

BY THE END OF August the time of departure for many on the island drew near. Brigades of traders were preparing to travel to the western wilderness, *voyageurs* to their homes in the east, and the Indians to their winter hunting grounds. There were so many departures it was a wonder the island did not lift from the lake and float away in its new lightness. This year, with his farm to see to, Jacques would not be traveling with the traders. He made up for this by throwing himself into the departure preparations of the brigade of M. Gauthier and his Menomonee wife, Mme. Gauthier. The Gauthiers' canoe was packed with trade goods: tobacco, blankets, calicoes, silver, beads, guns, and traps. Stowed carefully under tarpaulins were baskets of flour and lard and lyed corn to feed the traders.

Jacques helped the Gauthiers choose four hardy *engagés* to make up their brigade. The *engagés* would do the paddling and the heavy portaging. "I picked the burliest men I could find," Jacques told me. The Gauthiers were among the last of the independents, and Jacques had not forgotten the trouble Brandson had given him for striking off for himself rather than joining Astor's American Fur Company. "When they get to their trading posts Brandson will send his brutes against them just as he sent them against me. I only wish I could be there to join the fight." Indeed, Jacques looked like he was ready to jump into a canoe.

Some days before the Gauthiers left, Little Cloud had appealed to James. "James, could you not draw one of your pictures of Red Fox for the Gauthiers to give to his Sauk grandparents?" Like Jacques, the Gauthiers would be trading with Little Cloud's father, Chief Black Wolf.

James immediately set to work happily crossing his eyes, sticking out his tongue, making mouselike squeaks and bearlike growls, all to keep Renard laughing so that his grandparents might see how happy he was. When he finished the portrait he made a second one to take with him to London so that Angelique might see her nephew. "And I shall send a picture of little Matthew to you," he promised.

While Jacques busied himself with the Gauthiers, White Hawk and I hastened to make use of the last warm days to harvest the corn. The carrots and parsnips would remain in the ground, covered with straw. As the days grew colder the roots would sweeten.

Little Cloud busied herself with the making of a cache pit to store her harvest of squash, pumpkins, and corn. Jacques offered to dig the pit, but Little Cloud said in her tribe it was a woman's job. The digging of it took her three days, and on the last day we could not see her at all. The pit was shaped like a fat bottle with a narrow neck. The neck was large enough so that Little Cloud could climb in and out. The pit was lined with dried grass. The floor of the pit was covered first with willow sticks and then with grass matting. Finally the dried corn and squashes were taken down and stored where they would be safe from the freezing weather that was sure to come. Little Cloud regarded her pit with great satisfaction. "There is no danger of our going hungry this winter," she said.

On the morning of the Gauthiers' departure Jacques and I went down to the shore to bid our old friends farewell and to wish them a successful journey. James joined us, for he meant to sketch the departing traders. White Hawk was there as well. He had been seeing off some friends from L'Arbre Croche. As the Gauthiers' boat pulled out, the brigade began to sing.

We were all busy waving to the Gauthiers and calling out our good wishes when I noticed another boat pulling out a quarter mile or so down the beach. "Jacques," I asked, "is there another brigade leaving today?"

Jacques looked puzzled. "No. I know of no other." After a moment he ran quickly up the side of the bluff for a better look. When he came down his face was stormy. With no word to us he hurried away, disappearing down Market Street.

When he returned he was carrying Papa's musket, a furious look on his face. "It's just as I thought," he said. "I made some inquiries. Brandson is sending four ruffians after the

Gauthiers. He means to give the Gauthiers a scare so they sign up with Astor. He wants no independents out there as competition. He's not even waiting until they are out in the hunting grounds. He plans to attack them immediately. The Gauthiers will stop at Ile de Castor tonight. Those rogues will follow them and run them down there. They'll wait until it's dark and take them by surprise."

Ile de Castor—Beaver Island as the English called it—was a large island a day's paddle from Michilimackinac. There had always been a few scattered tribes of Indians on Beaver Island, but most of the island was uninhabited.

"What can they do?" James asked. "Surely they won't murder the Gauthiers in their sleep."

"There will be no murder," Jacques said. "They will destroy the Gauthiers' canoe and throw their trade goods in the lake. For a trader that's as bad as murder. I mean to go and warn the Gauthiers. My canoe is lighter than the canoe of Astor's men, and I know where the Gauthiers will camp. I have a good chance of getting there in time." I reached for Jacques, as if by clinging to him I could hold him back. In seconds he had pulled away and was running toward his canoe.

"Wait for me," White Hawk called. "Two can paddle a lot faster than one."

"And me!" James sprinted after Jacques and White Hawk.

They were like three boys on a lark instead of three men engaged in a dangerous mission against four bullies. I stood there helpless, watching as the three men pushed the canoe out into the water and climbed in, James a little awkwardly, for he was used to barges and ships rather than light canoes.

I gathered up my skirts, ran down to the beach, splashed though the water, and climbed into the canoe, nearly upsetting it.

James, Jacques, and White Hawk sat with open mouths, so surprised they allowed the canoe to move into deep water before they found their voices. "What do you think you're doing, Mary?" Jacques shouted at me. "The water here is too deep to pitch you out. You're going to make us lose time by having to turn around. I've a good notion to let you swim to shore."

"They are four of them," I said, "and there are only three of you. Four can do a better job of paddling than three. And I know how to shoot Papa's musket."

"Nonsense, Mary," James said. "We must

take you back at once. It's no job for a lady." I believe he was thinking of the time on board ship when I had climbed to the top of the mast and would not come down until the captain had slung me over his shoulder.

White Hawk was grinning. "Mary has tracked down grave robbers and captured ruffians bent on stealing her cow. Let her stay. I'm sure she will discover a way to help us."

How I loved White Hawk for believing I was a help and not a hindrance. Before any further argument could be made I took up a paddle.

Apart from some glowering looks from Jacques and a worried frown from James, no more was said. We saved our breath for our work. The island of Michilimackinac grew smaller and smaller. The light canoe skimmed over the water. It seemed barely to touch the lake. We kept paddling until my back and arms ached and I felt blisters on my hands. We stopped only for a moment or two to splash our faces and gulp some water.

The September sun slipped lower on the horizon, gilding the surface of the lake so that it looked as if we were paddling across the surface of the sun. Jacques had guided us in a direction he was sure the other canoe would not take. He had traveled this route with the Gauthiers and knew where on the island they would be stopping. "There's a cove on the south side of the island where Pierre and Marie set up camp. Astor's men will have to waste time paddling around the shore looking for them."

The golden lake turned purple and then dark blue. A cool breeze started up. In the east a sliver of moon played at hide-and-seek as clouds wandered across it and then floated away. We were silent now, for in the darkness we had no way of knowing whether anyone was near enough to hear us.

"Over there," White Hawk whispered. I could see that there was a campfire on the distant shore. I had thought I could not paddle another stroke, but finding the dancing light of a fire in all that darkness gave me strength. In no time we were pulling our canoe onto the shore, the wet sand firm under our feet, the fragrance of cedar and hemlock all around us.

Someone grabbed me around the throat. "Let us go, you fool!" Jacques cried. "It's only Jacques O'Shea." We were released, and led to a campfire where we found ourselves in the middle of a circle of surprised Gauthiers and their four *engagés*. A moment later we were wolfing down squirrel stew and telling our story.

Jacques vowed, "We mean to give them a welcome they won't forget."

"We could put out our campfire. That way they might not find us," Pierre said.

"If they don't discover your whereabouts here on the island they will only follow you to your next camp," White Hawk warned, "and we wouldn't be there to help. I think we should allow them to discover the camp, and when they do, we'll be ready for them."

Jacques said, "I remember a bog near here with a small island in the middle of it."

Marie nodded. "But what of it? We can't go there. We would be up to our waists in muck trying to reach that island."

White Hawk said, "I know what Jacques is getting at. We'll put out this campfire and build one on the island. They'll mistake the island for our camp and rush into the bog."

James's voice was full of excitement. "And we'll be ready for them!" He looked at me. His excitement turned to worry. "Mary, you should not be here."

White Hawk gave me an amused look. "James, you have much to learn about Mary." No further word was said about my presence.

After a glowing ember was plucked from the campfire, to light a torch, the fire was put out with lake water. Carrying the torch high over his head and spewing forth a stream of angry French, one of the *engagés* waded through the soft bog mud to the island, built a fire, and waded back. A minute later he was in the lake, trying to wash off some of the bog's muck.

After that we kept silent. When the clouds crossed the moon we couldn't see one another, but when the clouds drifted off we made a strange picture. There was Pierre with his face nearly hidden by his long black hair, and Mme. Gauthier, as tall and strong as any man there. Jacques was grinning in anticipation of the fight to come, while White Hawk appeared serious and patient. The four *engagés* were hardy men who had tested themselves a hundred times against the perils of the wilderness. James looked about, memorizing a scene that would one day, I was sure, become a painting.

White Hawk reached for my hand and put a small hatchet into it. I gasped. I hated Astor's men, but I thought a good pounding would do for them. I knew I could never chop off their heads.

"It's for their canoe, Mary," White Hawk

reassured me. "The minute we hear them come up the beach you are to follow the shore and discover where they have left their canoe. When you finish with it there should be no question of their leaving here until they have built a new boat. By then the Gauthiers will be far away."

I was relieved that I would be using the hatchet on a canoe and not on one of Astor's bullies. I saw by his frown that James was unhappy with my part in the scheme, but he would not risk another rebuke from White Hawk.

We huddled together in the little copse of hemlock and cedar trees, guarding the canoe and the trade goods. The moon's narrow horn climbed nearly to the top of the sky before we heard whispers. Four dark shadowy shapes moved along the beach. The whispers sounded so close I was afraid Astor's men would hear us, though it seemed that in the excitement we had all stopped breathing.

"They've built their campfire up in the woods," one of the men hissed. "They'll be lying asleep around the fire. We'll take them by surprise, tie them up, and then we can do what we like with their trade goods and canoe."

The four men moved slowly toward the fire, thinking they were on safe ground. The next minute we heard splashing noises and gurgles as the men thrashed about in the bog. White Hawk gave me a little push. "Now, Mary, quickly. Go and find their canoe."

As I ran I could hear blood-curdling screams from the Gauthiers and their *engagés* and loudest of all from Jacques, White Hawk, and James as they fell upon the intruders, who were trying to struggle out of the bog.

I followed the curve of the beach, searching in the darkness for the canoe. Then the clouds parted, revealing the canoe in the distance. Next to it was a dark shadow. I halted, terrified that one of the men had stayed to guard the canoe. I made myself take a step forward and then another, not daring to breathe. No one jumped out at me. As I got closer to the canoe I saw it was pulled up beside a huge chunk of driftwood that had looked in the darkness like some monster standing guard. It was no work at all to hack great holes in the birch bark. All canoes are made as light as possible so that they can be more easily carried in portages. When I had finished with it I knew that no one would paddle that canoe again. Before Astor's men could leave Beaver Island they would have to take the time to build a new canoe.

I hurried back along the shore, uncertain

of what I would find. I knew the evil men were outnumbered, but they were strong and were surely armed with knives and muskets. What I found were four very wet and enraged men neatly tied into packages. Their language was most unpleasant. I assured everyone that I had thoroughly demolished the canoe, whereupon the men's language grew even worse, and James put his hands over my ears.

"Mr. Brandson will undoubtedly reimburse you for your canoe," Jacques told the packages. "I have no question but that he was the one who sent you on this little errand."

By now we were all tired and hungry. A new campfire was lit, and we feasted on bowls of pea soup and stick bread made by mixing flour with water, molding the dough onto sticks, and roasting it over the fire. When we finished with our dinner, blankets were laid down. With the men securely tied, we were ready to drift safely off to sleep. When the curses did not stop, James heaved a pail of cold water in their direction. "Mind your manners," he said. "There are ladies present." After that all was quiet.

In the morning Pierre made a batch of pancakes, which we had with maple syrup. The four men watched hungrily at our show of savoring each bite. When the canoes were packed we bid the Gauthiers' brigade another farewell. They pushed off in their canoe. We settled in our own canoe while the four men watched us, terrified of being left tied up upon the island with no help at hand. Just as we were about to leave, White Hawk cut the cord that bound the hands of one of the men. The man was working on the knots that bound his legs as we paddled away and gaily waved our farewells.

The return to Michilimackinac was more leisurely than our going over had been. There was much singing. James taught us sailing songs while White Hawk contributed war chants, and Jacques had an endless number of French songs learned from the *engagés* he had traveled with. My own contribution was the Irish ballads that Papa used to sing to us. And so we made our cheerful way home.

Our little expedition rekindled James's love of adventure. His urgings upon me to marry him and leave Michilimackinac were more frequent and more urgent. He could find little else on the island to amuse him. While White Hawk and I prepared the farm for winter, James tramped about restlessly with his sketchbook, eager to leave the island. I tried to imagine leaving with James, but I could not. All the days White Hawk and I had worked on the farm had bound us even closer. The trip to Beaver Island stayed in my mind. I believed that James, for all his adventurous spirit, would expect his wife to disport herself like a lady, while White Hawk, who had lived among the hardy island women and the women of his tribe, was more ready to let me do all I wished.

James still spoke of the time when I would sail with him for England, but he seemed less sure than before. I believed that seeing me on Beaver Island with White Hawk, he had guessed where my heart lay. White Hawk was willing to face a battle, but James was more temperate. He might be spirited in pursuing a woman, but he would not fight for her. Fighting for something or someone had never been necessary for him. His life had been too easy. After all his travels and adventures he would have his same comfortable home to return to. He knew he would never want for anything.

As he and Emma set off each day with their sketchbooks and paints, he never looked back. He enjoyed Emma's company. One afternoon after she had left he said, "You American girls say what you think. That's a great blessing and enjoyment for a fellow."

I began to suspect that James found American girls as interchangeable as sparrows in a flock. If I was not available, Emma would do. At first such a thought angered me. I was ashamed to find myself jealous of Emma. I scolded myself, telling myself if I could not say yes to James's proposal, I should not mind if he looked Emma's way. Still my vanity was hurt. Hadn't James made me an offer on the roof of Castle Oakbridge? Hadn't he sailed across the ocean after me? Yet the more I thought about it, the more I felt that had she been on the roof with him he would have made the same offer to Emma, and that his sailing across the sea was just one more adventure.

James still asked me daily to be his wife and go away with him, but each day his request was less urgent, and at times he hardly waited for an answer, so sure was he of hearing my usual refusal.

I sensed James was becoming restless. He made no further efforts to become a farmer, and even the sketching began to bore him. It was only Emma's company that took him out each day. “I’ve pretty much seen all there is to see on Mackinac,” he said. “Jacques has promised to take me to St. Joseph Island one day.”

I smiled and agreed such a trip would be of interest. I knew, though, that White Hawk would never say he had seen all there was to see on this island. White Hawk and I could not walk five feet in the woods without stopping a dozen times to exclaim over a new kind of moss or the color of a mushroom. I wondered whether James would be a truly great artist if he tired so soon of looking at what lay about him.

One day I was high in an apple tree reaching for the bright red fruit that hung from the top branches when I saw James looking about for me.

“Up here,” I called, “and catch the apples as I throw them.”

James looked about for a moment, puzzled, until he spotted me. “Throw away, but don’t go any higher. There’s no Captain Hodge to carry you down from there, Mary.”

When the last apple was captured, I gathered my skirts about me, ready to descend from the tree, when James called to me, “Wait, Mary, I’m coming up.”

Climbing the tree was nothing to James after his years of scrambling up and down masts. In a moment he had settled beside me on a thick branch of the old tree.

"Mary, do you remember when you and I were together on the roof of Castle Oakbridge?"

I remembered it well and thought now of how from that height James and I had looked out at the castle's parks and gardens, its pastures and fields.

"Do you remember, Mary, how I asked then if you would be my wife and live with me at Oakbridge? You must know when I said at Oakbridge that I would be honored to have you be my wife I spoke with my whole heart. I have asked many times since then, but I have lost hope. Was I not right to have done so?"

I could only nod my head.

"And, Mary, I have not wanted to ask before because I did not want to hear the answer, but I would be very foolish and blind as well not to see that you and White Hawk care for one another. Now I must ask, am I wrong to believe this?"

"You are not," I said in a very quiet voice. I knew that the choice had long been made in my heart.

James said no further word, but climbed

down silently and walked away. I stayed on my perch watching James, a tear sliding down my cheek. James was very dear to me, but not so dear as White Hawk. When I could no longer see James, I looked out from my leafy height across the tall pines of the island at the two lakes that joined one another. There was no castle on the island, but no princess could have loved her kingdom more than I.

One late September afternoon Mrs. West labored up the path to pay a call on me. She looked about the cabin in her usual critical way, as if she were there to make a report on all she saw. At last she sat down on the edge of a chair as if she feared that it would soil her dress, although in fact the chair had just been dusted. She sat with her feet neatly placed together and her hands folded primly in her lap. "I am sorry to say, Mary, that Mr. Brandson has seen Emma about the island, sketching with that Lindsay person. Of course I have no objection to her perfecting her talent, but I don't think it is suitable for her to spend time alone with him. I have told her the lessons must cease. I'm sorry to say that I must hold you responsible for bringing the two of them together, and now I must ask that you do your best to keep them apart."

"I'm sorry, mam, that you have this worry, but James cannot be bad for Emma. I think he is an honorable man. I wouldn't know how to keep them apart. I am in no position to give orders to either of them."

Mrs. West bristled at what I'm sure she regarded as impertinence. "I don't ask that you give orders, Mary, but I ask that you do not encourage an association that can only be an embarrassment to us all. Mr. Brandson, as you know, is fond of Elizabeth, but he would not want to be a part of a family in which one of the daughters of the house is imprudent." With that Mrs. West rose to leave, shaking her skirts as if dust had been swirling about the cabin and had settled on her.

The next day James appeared looking sheepish. He stood silent at the doorway and would not meet my eye. I had never known him to be without words, but now when I invited him in he glanced about in a strange way. When I told him to sit down he regarded the chairs as though he had never before sat in one. "James," I exclaimed, "whatever is the matter with you? Are you ill?"

With much clearing of his throat and much twisting of his hat, which he held awkwardly in his hands, James blurted out, "Mary, you will not be angry if I tell you that I mean to ask Emma to be my wife, will you?"

I wished James well with all the warm feeling I could manage. We laughed together over the surprise in store for Mrs. West.

James said, "She has forbidden me to see Emma, for she says a poor artist is not suitable for her daughter. What will she say when the truth is known?" As he left, James gave me a sad look. "We will always be friends, Mary, will we not?"

"How could we not?" I asked. "But James, there is something that you must have." I opened the small box in which I kept my few treasures and took out the brooch James had given me. Emeralds and sapphires had been fashioned into forget-me-nots.

James refused to take it. "No, Mary. Nothing would make me more unhappy than to have you fling it back at me."

"I'm not flinging it, James. It's not fair to Emma for me to keep it."

"I have told Emma all about us, Mary. When she comes to Oakbridge as my bride she will have the Lindsay jewels, great heaps of them. If she were to wear them all at once their weight would make her sink right through to the dungeon. I had the brooch made for you, and you must keep it as a pledge of our friendship."

He was so earnest I could not refuse, and we parted with a friendly handshake. After James left I put the brooch back in the little box next to Mama's silver cross and the blue beads White Hawk had given me. I would not admit to myself that I was sad at losing James. Instead I tried to tell myself I was only a little unhappy that Oakbridge, with its barns and stables and pens of fine pigs and cows and sheep, would never be mine.

CHAPTER 8

THE NEXT DAY, WHEN Emma ran up the path and burst into my cabin, too breathless to speak, I settled her on a chair and waited until she caught her breath. "Oh, Mary," she said, speaking in a quavering voice but unable to stop once she started, "what am I to do? James has asked me to marry him, and I have said yes. How could I not? He is so handsome and so funny and so kind and with such nice manners. There is no one on the island like him. The men here think only of how many animals they can kill and the money they will make in the doing of it. I know of no other man who would sit quietly in the woods with a sketchbook open upon his knee. But Mama has said she will murder me if I marry James."

"Emma, your mama may be angry, but surely she has not said she will murder you."

"I have never seen her so angry, and Elizabeth as well. My sister says I will ruin her chance of marrying Mr. Brandson with my foolishness. She says he will have nothing to do with our family if I lower myself to marry a poor artist."

"And what does James say?"

Emma looked at me. "That's what's so strange. He only smiles and says it will all turn out well, but I don't see how. Mama hissed and shouted at him and nearly threw him out of the house, and all the while James was smiling as if he had a secret."

Emma was miserable and Mrs. West in a temper. It was time for the truth. If James would not tell it, I would. "James is at fault, Emma," I said. "I understand why he is silent, but now I believe it is time I spoke with your mother."

Emma gave me a worried look. "I don't think she will see you, Mary. She is very angry with you for introducing James into our society."

I paid no attention to Emma but searched out my letters from Angelique, which I kept tied with a blue ribbon. I slipped them into my pocket. Taking Emma by the hand, I pulled her after me. Down the path we went to Market Street and the Wests' home, Emma resisting me all the way. I was the victor, because I had been hoeing and scything while Emma had lifted nothing heavier than a pencil.

An angry Elizabeth met us at the door. "I am surprised that you show yourself at our home, Mary. You had best keep away from Emma after this. You have been a bad influence upon her. Mr. Brandson says James Lindsay means to snatch away Emma's dowry and then run off and leave her."

"Indeed you have been reckless, Mary." Mrs. West bustled to the door, looking as ruffled and flustered as my hens had been when the lice had nipped at them. "It is only our long friendship with your dear papa that keeps me from shutting the door in your face. I have reminded myself that you have been raised without a mama and perhaps know no better."

I felt my face growing red, and my hands trembled. "Though Mama died when I was a baby, Papa ever kept her high principles before us. We always knew what Mama would have expected of us. Neither Mama nor Papa would have judged a man as you have judged James. Though she came from a noble family, Mama married my papa when he had no money at all, because he was noble in his behavior." That should have been all that was said, and what I said afterward should not have been said. It was like throwing fat on fire. "What's more," I foolishly went on, "Mr. Brandson has cheated the Indians and has no right to judge James Lindsay, or anyone else."

I believe Elizabeth would have torn me apart as the lions tore the Christians if Emma had not shielded me and pleaded, "Mary, please go away. You are only making things worse." Elizabeth pulled Emma inside.

Mrs. West was about to close the door in my face. "Leave at once, Mary. And know that you will not be welcome in this house again."

At that I came to my senses. Hastily I said, "The only thing James is guilty of is making mischief. He wished to be accepted for what he was and not for his family and fortune. I am sure he meant to tell you the truth soon."

Mrs. West drew herself up. "Family? Fortune?

That is nonsense. I suppose the truth is he has run away from the law in England after having disgraced himself."

"Oh, Mama," Emma begged. "Don't say such a thing."

"No, indeed," I said. "Lord Lindsay has only run away from his father, the Duke of Oakbridge, and his mother, the duchess. He has run away from their great home in London, Lindsay House, and their castle, Oakbridge."

Mrs. West was very pale. "Mary, you were ever one for stories, but this is shameful. You must have taken leave of your senses. How can you say such preposterous things? You are a very bad girl to make up such nonsense."

I took a deep breath. "I do have a story to tell you, and you must listen. May I come in and sit down, for it will take a while." There must have been something in my voice and demeanor that made them take me seriously in spite of their disbelief. Mrs. West motioned me inside and sank down upon a chair, waiting for me to begin. I told them how I had met James on the British ship *Comfort*, on which he was a midshipman, and then how Angelique and Mrs. Cunningham and I had met him again in London at Somerset House, where I had learned that James was the son of the Duke of Oakbridge. I described the fashionable parties at Lindsay House, with its sweeping stairway and elegant rooms. I told of my visit to Castle Oakbridge, with its majestic towers and miles of park. I said nothing of the reason for my visit other than to talk of the kindness of the duchess, Lady Elinor.

I believe the story was so pleasant to their ears that they wished to believe it but so incredible that they could not. "Here is proof," I said. I showed them Angelique's letters with her story of James's travels across the wilds of America and the mention of the duke and duchess and Castle Oakbridge.

Mrs. West looked at me suspiciously. "You could have written those letters," she said.

"No, Mama, never," Emma said, pointing to Angelique's graceful script. "Mary's handwriting looks like the beach after the gulls have been tramping over it. It must be true." Emma looked frightened. A moment earlier she had believed James loved her and that she had only her parents and Elizabeth to fight. Now there were castles and great houses looming up before her. With a sigh she said, "I'm afraid James has been having fun at my expense. He cannot have meant his proposal. I would never fit into the life you describe, Mary."

Elizabeth was quick to say, "Indeed, you are right, Emma. What Mary has done is even worse than putting you in the way of a poor artist, for she has allowed Lord Lindsay to trifle with your affections. A duke and duchess would certainly not welcome a simple girl from the wilds of America as a bride for their son."

"You are both wrong," I said. "I know very well that the duke and Lady Elinor would be very fond of Emma. How could they not be? They only want James to return and take up his responsibilities. If his marriage to Emma is the means of his return, they will welcome her with open arms."

Elizabeth gave me a searching look. "You sound very sure of that, Mary," she said.

I felt myself flush, but I managed to keep my voice light, for I had no intention of letting them guess that the duke and duchess had once welcomed me for that very reason. "James's parents are warm and kindly people, not haughty as they might be in their position."

Mrs. West said, "If what you say is true, Mary, Lord Lindsay was very wrong to mislead us. I will be severe with him."

In spite of her threat I could see that Mrs. West was full of pleasure and eager for so advantageous a match, while Elizabeth sat with her lower lip stuck out, pouting over her sister's good fortune. Mr. Brandson did not have a castle.

"You need not treat him severely," I said. "I have a better way to repay his foolishness."

"What can you mean?" Mrs. West asked.

"You could have your own little jest."

The three women looked at me with interest.

Later in the afternoon, when James appeared with his tangled hair and beard, his torn and soiled clothes, and the twinkle in his eye that showed how much he was enjoying his little joke, we were ready for him. We sat with needle and thread in our fingers and on our laps, skins and furs I had hastily borrowed from Jacques and Little Cloud.

"What are you up to?" James asked, puzzled at our industry.

"Mama has kindly assented to our marriage," Emma said. "We are sewing clothes to wear after our marriage."

"Yes," Mrs. West said, "I have agreed against my better judgment, Mr. Lindsay. Now we are making deerskin dresses so that Emma may accompany you on your journeys into the wilds."

"There will be a nice warm fur rug as well," Elizabeth said, "so that you may sleep out in the snow and ice with no bad effect."

"I had thought to give my daughters fine china as a part of their dowry," Mrs. West told James, "but now we think it more sensible to buy a few birch bark baskets from the Indians, though Emma shall have a kettle to carry with her."

"I hope you will allow me a kettle, James," Emma said turning her great brown eyes upon him. "I will need it to boil up porcupines and skunks and suchlike for our dinners."

James appeared bewildered. All of this was said with such earnestness that he could only believe they were serious. With much clearing of his throat and much twisting of his hat, which he pushed from hand to hand, James said, "I'm afraid I have made a great fool of myself. I thought to have proved something to myself, but instead I find I have made much mischief. Emma will have no need of your skins and furs and no need of a kettle."

I could not restrain myself. "Oh, James, how cruel you are to send Emma off into the wilderness with no skins and furs and kettle!"

James gave me a long look. "Ah," he said. "I see it all now. Mary has told you everything." He sank down on a chair.

"Indeed I have, James, and with good reason. You have made everyone miserable with your pretense. While you were playing your little game, everyone else was in ill temper and tears."

James hung his head. "I suppose you are furious with me, Mrs. West, and rightly so. I am sure you wish me out of your house and out of your sight forever." He got up.

Mrs. West did not wish Lord Lindsay of Lindsay House and Castle Oakbridge out of her house, but she did not wish to show her eagerness. "You may sit back down, James. You have been a very naughty boy at our expense, but I put it down to high spirits and I forgive you."

James still appeared troubled. "Emma, it is you I have harmed the most with my charade. Can you ever forgive me?"

Emma smiled up at him. "You are already forgiven, James, but I'm afraid my simple clothes will look like skins and furs to the fashionable world of London."

"Nonsense. Mary will tell you our life at Oakbridge is a simple one. Besides, nothing would give my mother more pleasure than to take you about to the shops. You shall have as many ruffles, pleats, lace, and feathers as you wish, though when you are alone with me I hope you will dress just as you dress now. Nothing could be more becoming."

After that there was much talk of wedding plans. It was clear that Mrs. West meant to have a wedding suitable for the son of a duke. As the menu was planned and the list of guests grew and grew I saw that James was uncomfortable. I guessed that he yearned for a simple ceremony, wishing for nothing better than a quiet wedding and a quick departure with Emma from the island. Mrs. West, however, would not be deprived of celebrating to its fullest her daughter's fine catch. As the planning went on I quietly made my escape. My last sight was of the miserable expression on James's face as Mrs. West inquired whether he and Emma would be required to wear crowns during the wedding ceremony.

When I returned to the farm I bustled about, cutting herbs to dry for the winter: rosemary and thyme for seasoning, lavender to tuck amongst the linens, and peppermint for stomachaches. I readied my boots for fall, polishing them with lampblack. I mended a hole in the pasture fence and made a pretty blue ball of flannel for Renard to toss about. When I had done all that, I could think of nothing more to keep myself busy. I stood looking out at the lake where the small brigades of traders had headed west toward Prairie du Chien and Fond du Lac and the wilderness beyond.

My busyness had been intended to keep me from thinking of James and Emma. I knew I could never marry James. I knew where my heart lay. Still, I could not quite rejoice in their happiness, and for that I scolded myself. James and Emma would sail to England to begin their new life, while I would remain on the island. As much as I loved the island and White Hawk, I could not be sure that White Hawk would always be there with me. When he was away, what would I do? There was little farming to keep me busy during the long winters.

I wanted to give myself some peace and was making a great effort to put the marriage out of my mind when I saw Emma come up the path. If I were not sure that she had already seen me I would have hidden myself in the haystack. Selfish as it was, I was not yet ready to enjoy her happiness or to hear a discussion of her plans for her wedding to James.

It was not with a happy face that she greeted me. Instead she looked most serious. "Emma, is something wrong?" I wondered whether James had fled to escape Mrs. West's elaborate arrangements.

"No, Mary. Nothing is wrong, but you and I must have a talk."

"You look so serious. I hope I have done nothing to cause you trouble."

Emma took my hand and gently led me to the doorstep, where she pulled me down to sit. "Mary, I know that James loved you."

"Emma! What are you saying? James loves you."

"Yes, I believe he does, at least a little. If I didn't believe that, much as I love him I would not marry him. But first, Mary, he loved you."

Startled, I said, "Surely James has not told you such a thing."

"He has only said that you and he had been great friends in England and that he had once been fond of you. But Mary, I saw how he looked at you when he first came to the island. And there was your visit to Castle Oakbridge. How could he care for you and still care for me?"

"Emma, though you never said anything, I saw that you cared for Jacques. Isn't that so?"

For a long time Emma was silent. At last she nodded her head. "That was a long time ago,

Mary. Jacques is married to Little Cloud and has a son. I haven't thought of him as I used to in a very long time."

"You are certain you no longer care for him?"

"Very certain. I love James," she said, "no one else."

"Why shouldn't it be the same for James, Emma? It's true that he might once have thought kindly of me, but that's in the past. He loves you now, just as you love him."

Emma smiled. I don't know whether she truly believed me or only wished to believe me, but whichever it was, she went away happy. I wondered whether she realized that many of the same qualities that she had admired in Jacques—his impulsiveness, his easy laughter, his whole-heartedness—were a part of James as well. It pleased me that those were the things Emma loved about James and not his castle and riches.

That same evening White Hawk came racing up the hill to the farm. Trying to catch his breath and talking at the same time, he managed to ask, "Mary, is it true? Are James and Emma to be married?"

I laughed at the expression on his face.

"Yes, it's true."

"And, Mary," he said, looking closely at me, "what do you think of such an arrangement?"

"White Hawk, I could not be happier."

He searched my face and must have seen the truth there, for he reached for my hand.

The late September evening was like black silk. We watched the moon the Indians call Moon of the Yellow Leaves rise over the lake, sending a path of dancing gold across the lake. So peacefully quiet were we, sitting hand in hand, that a great gray owl settled down on a nearby pine branch. It was rare to see the gray owl so far south. In the light of the moon we could see it ruffle its feathers and then fold in its wings. We held our breath lest we frighten the owl away. We needed no more words than the magical presence of the owl to express our happiness at being safe and together and at home on our island.

CHAPTER

9

JAMES AND EMMA'S WEDDING was planned for early October so that they would have time to make the long journey across the country to New York before the snows grew deep. From New York they would sail to London. Often in the days before the wedding I found myself daydreaming of Angelique and Daniel and my nephew, little Matthew, and their cozy house in St. John's Wood. I longed to see them and half wished I might be making the trip myself.

It took only a walk with White Hawk to send my yearnings flying. Set against a blue sky, the gold birches shimmered and the red maples burned. The fields were purple with wild asters and gilded with goldenrod, just as they had been on the day of Angelique's wedding. Overhead hundreds of circling hawks would soon make their way south. We stretched out on our backs in the hay field, the better to see them. There were big hawks and small ones, hawks with red tails and hawks with red wings. They hovered and plunged and wheeled, they glided and spiraled until the sky boiled up with them. I thought of the eagle I had seen caged in London and all the people there shut into their houses with only parks to walk in and no woods at all, and I was content.

As we watched I said to White Hawk, "Those are your namesakes above us. Will you fly south like those hawks and leave us?"

He sat up and brushed the hay from his jacket and hair. "I wish I could say, no, Mary. I wish I could promise I would never leave the island again, but I cannot. My people at L'Arbre Croche need me. But Mary, L'Arbre Croche is only a day's paddle away. I am hoping you will be often with me there. My people haven't forgotten your plan for catching the grave robbers. They respect you, Mary, and want to make you a part of the tribe.

"And when I'm on the island, Mary, you will have to chase me away from the farm, for I mean to give you all the help you need."

White Hawk was as good as his word. He pruned the tangle of raspberry bushes and gathered the apples, climbing to the tops of the trees and pitching down every last one to me. Together we manured the fields so that the soil would be rich in the spring. We cut the bracken that had browned and dried until it looked like shriveled hands. The bracken would be used for bedding for my two pigs. The third pig was already butchered, salted, and hanging in Mr. MacNeil's smokehouse. We spent a brisk day under rolling clouds gathering acorns in the woods for the pigs' winter fodder, taking care that the acorns were this year's, for pigs choke upon old and hard acorns. All the while I worked I wondered how I was to get through the days when White Hawk was away from the island. I knew that to keep from brooding, I must find some useful work.

While White Hawk and I hurried to finish the last tasks on the farm before the icy winds blew over the island, the Wests hurried to complete arrangements for the wedding. The day of the wedding was crisp, with a clear blue sky. Some days before, Little Cloud and I had rummaged through my trunk of London dresses. Little Cloud was so taken with all the finery, she decided she would put aside her calico and deerskin for one day. She chose a pale blue silk dress with a high waist, a sweep of ruffle at the hem, and a frill of ruffle at the neck. The sleeves were tight, with puffs at the shoulders. I braided her black hair and pinned the braids into graceful loops. She could not have looked more elegant.

My own choice was more plain, a pale green chintz with a pattern of small roses and a shirred bodice, the whole set off by a dark green taffeta sash.

Little Cloud saw that Jacques's hair was combed and his boots cleared of mud. He and White Hawk were both in fine jackets, breeches, and pleated shirts with stocks wrapped so tightly about their necks they complained that they would choke to death and never live to see the wedding at all.

So that we might arrive at the church with clean slippers and no briar rips or burrs on our finery, we hired old Mr. Blimpkin's cart and horse and so arrived at the church in style. The cart had carried pigs and chickens, so that we women had to mind our skirts and the men their breeches, but upon our arrival we were still presentable.

Pere Mercier had lent the church to Mrs. West's brother, Reverend Pritchard, a Methodist preacher who had come from Detroit to preside at the wedding. There was a bad moment when Mrs. West recalled that Reverend Pritchard frowned upon spirits. What was to be done with the casks of wine waiting in the West home for the festivities? It was decided that the wine would be referred to as grape juice, which indeed it had once been.

James was scarcely recognizable. His beard was gone, and his fair curls were pulled back neatly with a ribbon. He wore white satin breeches, shoes with silver buckles, a jacket with velvet lapels, and a silk ruffled shirt. Even at the most formal party in London he had not been so splendid. When he saw me staring, for I could not help it, he looked about to be sure Mrs. West was not in hearing distance. "You see what they have done to me, Mary. They have sent away for these ridiculous clothes and dressed me up like a monkey. After so much trouble I could not refuse to put on their ornaments, but the moment we are safely on the ship they will go overboard." He looked fondly in Emma's direction. "If I am ridiculous, just see how lovely my bride is."

Indeed she was. Emma hurried over to embrace us. Her white satin dress was embroidered with small pearls. Her hair was simply done and covered with a lace veil. Behind her we could see Mrs. West, got up in gray silk, and Elizabeth upholstered in a purple satin that caused her red complexion to look bruised. Resting on her head was a hat with so many plumes and feathers I was sure no bird would ever fly again. Hovering near her was Mr. Brandson, who glowered at us. He was stiffly dressed in a black coat, black breeches and stockings, and a very tall black hat. I whispered to Little Cloud that he was thrifty and had bought clothes that would do for both a wedding and a funeral.

Word had gone about the island that Emma was marrying royalty, the islanders making no great distinction between a duke and a prince, so much of the town crowded around the church to see the show. The reception at the Wests' home was a smaller affair. The MacNeils were there, and the commander of the fort, Captain Pierce, attended with his wife, Josette. Josette's mother,

Mme. LaFramboise, was also there in full Indian dress. Lieutenant Brady was there with his elegant French wife. The officers looked splendid in their blue coats and white breeches. Forgotten were those hard years of war when an English flag flew over Fort Michilimackinac and English guns were turned on American soldiers. On this day the officers had only friendly things to say as they toasted Emma's Englishman.

The table was set for a feast with great platters of roast venison, ham from Mr. MacNeil's smokehouse, wild ducks served with their tail feathers stuck back in, and a gift from Jacques and Pere Mercier, whitefish that had been stuffed with bread sauce and baked. There were apple and squash pies and on the sideboard a great Queen's cake, which James cut with a sword.

When we had done with the food and were as stuffed as the whitefish and sure we could not move, M. André and his friends took up their fiddles and played lively gallops and quadrilles. James danced a hornpipe, and Mr. MacNeil led a Scottish reel. Mr. Brandson managed a waltz with Elizabeth. Even Pere Mercier tucked up the skirts of his cassock to show us a French dance. At first the somber Mr. Pritchard had frowned upon the dancing, but after he had drunk a few glasses of "grape juice" he demonstrated a very creditable jig.

In all the jollity a tiny worm nibbled at my pleasure in the celebration. I could not help thinking that unlike Emma, if I should marry, I would have no Mama and Papa by my side.

As always White Hawk guessed my mood. He stopped me as we were gliding over the parlor floor and said, "It is like the inside of a barrel here, Mary. Let's go outdoors where we can take a breath or two."

I gladly followed him out onto Market Street. The lake stretched as far as we could see, the waves slapping against the shore nearly drowning out the sound of violins and the stamping of feet. Above the town the bonfires lit by the soldiers illuminated the white walls of the fort. A northwestern breeze carried the fragrance of the distant pine trees to us.

White Hawk took my hand. "Mary, I've seen a sadness in your eyes tonight. Do you still care for James? Do you regret refusing him?"

I could honestly say, "I care deeply for James as a friend. But that is all. I am truly happy for Emma and James. I was only thinking that should I ever marry, I would have no Mama and Papa to help me celebrate."

"Be my wife, Mary, and you shall have all the Ottawa tribes to make you a feast."

"Nothing would please me more," I said with a smile, but as I looked up at him I saw that White Hawk was serious.

"Mary, with all my heart I want you to be my wife. Will you answer yes?"

I knew now that my heart had always been White Hawk's. "Yes," I said, "with all my heart."

His arms were around me. We slipped into the house just as Dr. West was calling for silence. "There is yet more good news this evening," he said. "It gives Mrs. West and me the greatest pleasure to announce that our Elizabeth and Ezra Brandson are pledged to one another and will be married at Christmastime."

Elizabeth was grinning foolishly, and Mr. Brandson was all puffed out. In his black suit he looked like a crow fluffing its feathers against a strong wind. We all applauded and cheered at the news. Emma and James congratulated Brandson and embraced Elizabeth. Toasts were proposed and drunk.

White Hawk whispered, "Shall we announce our news, Mary?"

"No," I quickly replied. "Even Jacques shan't know, for he has never been able to keep a secret in his life. As long as we are quiet about it, our secret will still belong to us. When it is told, it will belong to everyone." But I do not think it was a secret to everyone, for when I happened to glance over at James, he was watching us closely. Our flushed faces and our clasped hands must have told him much, for he gave me a knowing smile and a wink as if to say he was happy for us.

The next afternoon we bid farewell to James and Emma. Tears were shed all around, and Mrs. West vowed that after she had seen Elizabeth married she would come to London to see Castle Oakbridge for herself. I was sure that she was already planning her costumes. James and I exchanged a quick look, and he whispered to me, "I shall have the dungeon readied."

As we said our farewells Emma threw her arms around me and said, "Mary, I will never stop being grateful to you for bringing James here. Promise you will come to visit us. I only wish I had your courage to help me face my new life. I am sure I will do something to displease James's parents."

"Never, Emma. The duke and Lady Elinor will love you not only for bringing James back, but for your own goodness."

James also urged me to visit. With a sly smile he added, "And you must bring White Hawk." He pressed my hand warmly and turned to leave.

We watched as the little boat took Emma and James with their piles of boxes and trunks out to the schooner. After Emma was safely aboard I saw James clamber up the side of the ship. Immediately he began to stalk about the deck, poking into everything. He was a sailor once more. I was not so sure James would settle comfortably into the life of a London gentleman and a country squire. I recalled the day in London when he and I had visited the shop of the naturalist Charles Jamrach, where you might buy a box of tigers or a bag of dormice. James had shared my distress at the sight of a caged eagle. He had said, "I know how it feels to be caged when all I want in the world is to be let alone to make pictures." When he became master of Lindsay House and Castle Oakbridge, there would be little time for pictures. Poor James. Still, I was sure James and Emma would be happy.

White Hawk was talking with Ottawa friends who had come that day from L'Arbre Croche. Some new land trouble had come up. Little Cloud and Jacques had errands in the town. I walked up the path to the farm alone. A sharp northwest wind had started up. It would send James and Emma's schooner flying down Lake Huron. A tumble of maple leaves fell on me. The witch hazel was in bloom. Its spidery golden blossoms were always the last flower of the year. Only the day before I had seen a dozen yellow warblers flitting about in a bush. They were headed south. Soon the November fogs would wrap the island in cotton wool. Winter would come to the island and to the stubborn few of us who stayed on.

White Hawk and I had talked of our wedding, deciding it would be in the spring, when Mrs. Sinclair could come from Detroit for the ceremony. White Hawk had plans for improving the cabin. Together we visited L'Arbre Croche, where I received the congratulations of Chief Black Kettle. With a smile White Hawk translated the chief's words. "You must be sure White Hawk gives you your deer. No proper Indian girl would marry a brave who had not made her family a present of at least one deer to prove he was an able hunter."

CHAPTER 10

WITH WHITE HAWK'S HELP I hurried through the last tasks of autumn, planting clover in the potato field and storing Belle's winter supply of meadow grass in the stable. One day the cabin was perfumed with the lavender I steeped in water and mixed with lye and suet to make soap. The next day the cabin was fragrant with the cinnamon I used to season a kettle of apple butter.

We no longer had grass upon the ground.

There were no leaves upon the trees to shield us from the winds that wound around our island. When the lashings of a November storm overturned the boat of one of the fishermen, Pere Mercier read out the lesson of Jonah swallowed by the great fish. The great fish spit Jonah out on dry land, but no great fish spit out our fisherman, for his body was never found. A cross went up over his empty grave.

Snows fell on the island, covering houses and trees and turning fields and paths into empty white stretches. More wood was thrown onto the fire. Candles were lit earlier and burned later. I left a bowl of peas to soak overnight on the kitchen table. In the morning I found the water in the bowl frozen solid.

One morning I was sweeping away the snow from the paths to the henhouse and privy when I saw a solid white shape struggling through the swirling snow toward the cabin. It was White Hawk, coming to see whether I needed his help. Before letting him into the cabin I brushed him off with the broom until his snow-covered hair showed black once more and I could make out his jacket and boots.

We set mugs of cider to warm beside the fire and, as we often did on these winter days, took down a book of English poetry Angelique had sent. My first choice was Sir Walter Scott's poem about young Lochinvar who comes out of the west to rescue his beloved just as she is to be married to a cowardly bridegroom, "a laggard in love and a dastard in war." With tender feeling I read out the lines that tell how they make their escape:

One touch to her hand, and one word in her ear,
When they reach'd the hall-door, and the charger
stood near;

"If it's what you long for I would gladly come for you on my charger," White Hawk said. He had a small Indian pony, Raven, which Jacques and Little Cloud cared for.

"Raven would never hold the two of us," I said. "She would collapse into a heap, and we wouldn't get past the 'hall-door.'"

It was White Hawk's turn to choose a poem. With his deepest voice and with great expression, he read out Samuel Taylor Coleridge's lines:

In Xanadu did Kubla Kahn
A stately pleasure-dome decree:
Where Alph, the sacred river, ran
Through caverns measureless to man
Down to a sunless sea.

"Where is Xanadu?" I asked.

"Only in Coleridge's mind," White Hawk said, "and now in ours."

After a bit we put away the English poetry, and I stumbled through some lines of Virgil. White Hawk was teaching me Latin. "'*Latet anguis in herba*,'" he pronounced.

"*Herba* is grass, but you must give me another hint."

"*Anguis* is snake."

I ventured a guess. "A snake hides in the grass."

"Yes," White Hawk said, "but you needed too many hints. You're neglecting your studies." He sighed. "How much I would have missed without Pere Mercier's school."

"Why does Pere Mercier not teach girls as well?" I asked.

"I suppose it never occurred to him to teach girls."

"It's not right. There should be a school on the island for girls."

In jest White Hawk asked, "Then why don't you start one?"

"I will." The moment I made my reply I knew I meant what I said. I remembered that long ago I had told Little Cloud that I wished for some higher purpose. I had thought of something grand, but what could be better than a school for girls? "There are girls on the island who cannot read or write and never will unless someone teaches them."

"If you are to have a school then it must be in the winter, for in summer you'll never catch students. How will you get them to come in such weather as this?"

"I will find a way," I said. But in truth I didn't know.

In a week's time I had four students. The winter storms helped, for the girls were bored with keeping indoors with nothing to do, and their parents were glad to get the children out from under their feet. Knowing that more flies are taken with a drop of honey than a ton of vinegar, I had always some sweet cakes and a warm fire to greet my young pupils.

My four students were of mixed ages. Martha was seven, the daughter of a fisherman's family. She had a mop of brown curls and a high-pitched voice with which she questioned everything I said, and so much curiosity I had constantly to keep her from poking through my cupboards and trunks.

Aimée was nine, with long, straight black hair and a slender graceful body. Her mother was a Chippewa. Her French father had been a trader until a severe case of frostbite had crippled him. He now worked as a clerk in Mr. Astor's office. Aimée was a quiet child who watched everything I did, her brown eyes following my every move as if I had great secrets. At first she spoke only French, so that when they heard me translating for her, my other students picked up French words. Soon everyone could converse a bit in two languages.

Caroline was eleven, the daughter of one of the officers' families at the fort. She was plump as a well-fed hen and just as chatty. The family had traveled from fort to fort, and Caroline relished above all things telling the other girls stories of horrible bloody fights, complete with much scalping and chopping and shooting.

The oldest girl, Leah, was the daughter of a

farm family. She came to the school with equal amounts of embarrassment and eagerness, for she was fourteen, and afraid she was too old to learn to read.

The short winter days went quickly, for I was up early to finish my chores before my students arrived and up late to prepare the lessons for the next day. In addition to reading and writing I taught simple sewing, but Leah was a better seamstress than I was. My stitches were too large and wandered. I let her teach sewing, and the responsibility made her less conscious of her deficiencies in schoolwork.

One day, a week before Christmas, I gave my pupils cocoa and gingerbread, a rare treat during our Advent fast, before sending them home. As I watched the four girls racing one another down the hill I felt at last I had found the purpose I had sought.

The next days were spent in a flurry of cooking for *réveillon*. *Réveillon* was the feast that celebrated the end of the Advent fast. It was held after the midnight Mass on Christmas Eve. I was to provide the meal for Jacques, Little Cloud, Renard, and White Hawk.

Apples, venison, and suet needed to be

chopped for mincemeat pies. The neck of a hen wrung and the hen dipped into boiling water and plucked. Carrots and parsnips dug and scraped. Dried mushrooms and onions turned into a soup. Cornbread baked. The plum pudding soaked in brandy. Mama's recipe got out for tiny pancakes rolled with maple sugar.

White Hawk split wood for the fireplace and carried it into the cabin, heaping it high, for on these cold days the fire was never out. While he and Jacques went off in search of some hares for a stew, Little Cloud came to help, bringing Renard, who was walking now. He was a lively, curious child, who must sample every dish, so that his mouth was always full and his fingers always sticky.

Everyone on the island said it was the coldest Christmas season in memory. On the day of Christmas Eve great swaths of ice formed on the lake. The fog had hung in the trees the evening before. By morning the dampness was frozen into ice crystals, and the trees sparkled in the cold sun. Snow fell until it seemed there could be no more snow left. In the village they were busy shoveling paths from house to house, so that Market Street was a maze of narrow high-walled lanes.

On Christmas Eve, muffled and wrapped and carrying torches against the dark, we all made our way to St. Anne's. We hurried half frozen into the church so as not to let in the bitter winds. The church was a blaze of candlelight. Cedar boughs had been cut for decoration, and their fragrance filled the church. We all huddled close to share our warmth. Pere Mercier sang the familiar Christmas hymns in his native French. When the service was over, we hurried, slipping and sliding on the snowy path, back to the cabin. Below us we could see the torches of the townspeople as they hurried to their homes, and then one by one the houses came alive with the lights of lanterns and candles.

In my cozy cabin more wood was thrown on the fire. We all gathered around the table, all except Renard, who, even with all the food to tempt him, had fallen asleep. We heaped our plates with roast pig, squash sweetened with maple syrup, and carrots swimming in butter I had churned that morning. Just as we were about to settle into our feast there was a pounding at the door. Jacques poked his nose out into the darkness and then called to White Hawk, "It's someone from L'Arbre Croche." White Hawk coaxed his friend into the cabin, where he warmed himself gratefully at the fire.

I was the only one in the room who did not understand what the man was saying. Still, I could see that his words greatly troubled the others. When he left they settled around the table, but all the tasty food I had prepared went untouched.

"What is it?" I demanded.

Jacques looked very solemn. "White Hawk's friend is returning to L'Arbre Croche tomorrow and he wants White Hawk to come with him."

"That's impossible," I said, my heart squeezed tight in my chest. "In a few days the lake will be frozen over, and White Hawk will never be able to get back here."

"Black Kettle is calling for him to return," Little Cloud said. The tone of her voice suggested that no argument could be made against such a command.

White Hawk looked troubled. "Mary, I must go. You know the corn crop was poor this year, and what there was of it went to the fort and to Astor. The supplies of squash and peas and dried fish will never last the winter. In the old days the tribes would go down to hunt near the Grand River, but that land is being settled, and the game is nearly gone. They are facing starvation at L'Arbre Croche, and the chiefs who want to sell the Ottawas' land for money and food are saying that if they don't do so now the tribes will starve. I must make them understand that should the land be sold they would have money and food, but next year there wouldn't be enough land for planting corn." White Hawk looked troubled. "You know I am against the sale of land, but how can I stand by and see my people starve?"

I pointed to our table. "Why must they starve when we have food?"

White Hawk shook his head. "That's generous of you, Mary, but even this banquet would not last more than a day or two amongst so many people—and there is the whole winter ahead."

I hurried on. "I don't mean just this. Why can't we gather food from everyone on the island, from our friends, from the fort, even from Astor's fur company?"

Everyone looked at me. For a moment they were silent. Finally Jacques said, "Why not? Tomorrow is Christmas. Everyone will be in generous spirits, except the fur company. There is no point in counting on them."

A slow smile was spreading over White Hawk's face. "Yes," he said. "Yes. We'll try."

Early Christmas morning we scattered in all directions. Jacques hurried to the fort. Little Cloud went to see the MacNeils. White Hawk went to ask Pere Mercier to make an announcement at the Christmas morning service. I made my way to the Wests. They opened their door to me with great surprise, Mrs. West still in her wrapper and Dr. West without his wig. Only Elizabeth was properly got up. From the twists and fancy curls upon her head, I thought she must have sat up all night in her bed. Behind her was Ezra Brandson, who was spending the Christmas holiday as a guest of the Wests.

"Why, Mary!" Mrs. West said. "What brings you out at this time of day? Has something happened?"

"I'm sorry to bother you at such an early hour, but the Indians at L'Arbre Croche don't have enough food for the winter and are so desperate they think of selling their land for food, which would be a terrible thing. White Hawk is going there, and we want to send food with him. We are asking everyone to give something."

Though it was sometimes hidden by his stiff manner, Dr. West had a good heart, surely a fine thing in a doctor. Now he stepped forward. "You may count on us. We will explore our storeroom and see what we can contribute."

Looking at Mr. Brandson, who seemed to be hiding behind Elizabeth, I recalled Jacques's warning that little might be expected from the American Fur Company. I bestowed my sweetest smile on him. "Mr. Brandson, sir, how fortunate to find you here. When we heard the news last night your company was our first thought. 'Surely,' we all said, 'Mr. Astor would want the American Fur Company to contribute to this good cause.' We know your warehouse is always well supplied. Pray tell us, sir, what we may count on from you."

Mr. Brandson's face was a bright red. "Well, something, a very little, of course I cannot say for sure, but something might be done."

"But, sir," I said in an innocent voice, opening my eyes very wide, "surely you have great authority at the company and can tell us now what we may expect."

In a proud voice Elizabeth said, "Mr. Brandson, you have often told us there is no one on our island higher than you are in the company." The heads of all the Wests turned expectantly toward Mr. Brandson, and I saw that he was torn between his natural stinginess and his wish to be well thought of by his future in-laws. I guessed the need to display his own importance would win out, and I was right.

"Certainly, I may say what is to be given. I believe we have a barrel or two of lyed corn left from the supply we put in for the traders."

"Come, come, Mr. Brandson," Dr. West said. "You mentioned only last week that there were above fifteen barrels in the warehouse. Surely all the traders have long since taken off, and by next year would not the corn be moldy? After all, the corn came from L'Arbre Croche."

"Well, yes, it did, but we paid good money for it." He felt Dr. West's flinty gaze upon him. "Perhaps after all I might shift the barrels to the Indians, though why we should worry about savages I don't know."

My first impulse was to kick Mr. Brandson's shins and tell him what a fool he was and that if there were savages about they were not the Indians but men like himself. Yet I did not. Before my mind's eye were the barrels of corn and the thought of what they would mean at L'Arbre Croche. I bit back my angry words and said in my sweetest voice, "Oh, Mr. Brandson, how generous you are, and how grateful the Indians will be for your kindness to them."

Not to be outdone, Mrs. West said, "I have

some quite nice marmalade all the way from London. I would gladly send a jar or two, though it was most difficult to come by."

Dr. West smiled slightly and said, "That is kind of you, my dear, but I daresay the Indians have some maple syrup for sweetness, and they perhaps would find marmalade a bit strange. We have several crocks of rendered fat from the hogs' butchering. That will be of greater benefit in this cold weather."

I bobbed a curtsey to Mrs. West, bid Elizabeth and her fiancé farewell, gave Dr. West a great hug, and was on my way.

When we gathered at the church to find what our success had been, the news was cheering. The fort would send barrels of flour and salt pork, for Josette LaFramboise, who was married to Captain Pierce, was herself part Indian and in her childhood had seen hunger. The MacNeils had a fine bean crop and would send bushels of dried beans and a side of bacon from Mr. MacNeil's smokehouse. The announcement, coming as it did on the morning of Christmas when everyone was full of good food and good spirits, brought promises of contributions from all the congregation.

I saved my news for last. After church, when Jacques, Little Cloud, Renard, and White Hawk were in the cabin, I said, "Guess what Mr. Brandson is giving."

Jacques scowled. "A moldy piece of cheese or half a dead muskrat."

I smiled in a most superior way. "No indeed. He is giving ten barrels of lyed corn."

Until I told the whole story no one believed me. "Now, Jacques," I said, "you must be pleasant to him."

"He was shamed into it," Jacques said. "Still, when next I see him I will fall to my knees in prostration and reverence."

"There is no need for that," I said, laughing at the thought of such a sight, "only you must not fight with him ever again."

Later in the afternoon, when the others had left and White Hawk and I were alone, I said, "You must promise to hurry back. The lake already is half frozen over. Another week of such weather and there will be no returning from L'Arbre Croche until the spring."

White Hawk took my hand. "Mary, I must be honest. I can't say when I'll return. I have to stay until I am sure there is no more talk of selling land. If more land is lost it will be a disaster. Already there is hardly enough for the cornfields."

My heart sank. "You are talking of two or three months. How am I to get along without you?"

"I've already spoken to Jacques. He has promised to come each day to see how you are doing. He'll keep the paths open and split wood for you."

How could White Hawk believe that it was merely cleared paths and split wood that I desired? I was put out that he could not understand that it was himself that I would miss. I did not know how I could get through the long winter weeks without him. In my anger I answered him sharply. "Indeed, I'm sure I will do well without you."

White Hawk gave me a wounded look and soon left.

The next day, with a northwest wind and snowflakes so fine they were no more than a glimmer in the air, Little Cloud and I watched a fleet of canoes led by White Hawk and Jacques set off for L'Arbre Croche. The canoes were heaped with food.

Seeing my unhappiness at White Hawk's departure, Little Cloud said, "When our warriors left for battle we knew that some among them would not return to us. It is true White Hawk may be gone for some months, but, Mary, you can be sure he will return to you."

Little Cloud's gentle reminder of what little I had to complain about heaped hot coals upon my head. I would have given anything to take back my waspish words to White Hawk. Though I could not be as brave as the wives of the warriors, I knew I had to allow White Hawk to do what he thought right. I could not love him less because he loved his people.

Two days later when Jacques returned, White Hawk was not with him. "It was a close thing," Jacques said. "The ice formed so quickly that on our way back our canoes were nearly trapped. There will be no more canoes on the lake until spring." When he saw the miserable look on my face, Jacques said, "I nearly forgot, Mary. White Hawk sent you this note."

The first moment I had alone I tore it open.

Dear Mary,

Please do not think me a laggard in love. Though I am no Lochinvar, I mean to swoop down upon the island and carry you away to L'Arbre Croche as soon as spring comes. Until then, I send you my dearest love.

White Hawk

He had forgiven me my surliness. I saw that if I was to have White Hawk, I would also have farewells and returns. Just as the wives of the *voyageurs* saw their husbands leave in the fall for the waters of Superior, I, too, would be an island wife.

Christmas was over. The New Year came and went. I was happy to have my little school resume. There was much rejoicing when Leah could read out a whole sentence. Aimée's wariness could not withstand Caroline's friendly patter or Martha's ready questions. Huddled together around the fire while the cold winds shook the cabin, we grew close as family.

Even with all my busyness the days moved along slowly. The island was an enchanted white fortress locked in a spell of ice. I longed for open water with the impatience of someone dying of thirst.

CHAPTER

11

THE ICICLES THAT HAD decorated my cabin all winter disappeared drop by drop in the April sun. Beside the doorway the yellow and purple primroses poked up through the last patches of snow. The chickens ran about, cackling their pleasure at being outside. Late at night I could hear the thunder of ice cracking on the lake. Soon the fishermen were pushing their boats out into narrow channels of water running between the slabs of ice. Even in their eagerness none of the fishermen ventured far, for the blocks of ice could shift in a moment, trapping a boat and even crushing it.

Impatient for White Hawk's return from L'Arbre Croche, I had fancies of marching out onto the ice and chipping it away. Sunny days and warm winds did the work for me.

Early one April morning, just after my students had arrived, White Hawk burst into the cabin. Before any of us could say a word, he announced to the astonished students, "School is over. Miss O'Shea is going to leave today on a little journey." The girls looked at me. Blushing, I gave my permission. Hastily they gathered their things and, giggling and poking one another, left the cabin.

I looked closely at White Hawk. In a frightened voice I said, "Your face is so thin, and your clothes hang about you. Have you been ill?"

"I may weigh a pound or two less, but that is nothing." He brushed aside my concern and, after gathering me in his arms, said, "You must put together a few things. I want to take you back to L'Arbre Croche with me. We have to hurry. There is still ice out there, and a shift in the wind could push it our way."

"But I haven't said I would go with you. I

expect Belle to calve the end of the week. I must be here."

"I'll promise to have you back in time. Would you leave me to return alone when I have come all this way for you?" He looked very earnestly at me. "Besides, there is something you must see for yourself. It will tell a story better than all my words. While you get ready I'll let Jacques and Little Cloud know that you'll be gone for a few days. They'll see to the farm." His gaze fell upon a loaf of freshly baked bread. He tore it in two and ate half the loaf as quickly as if it had been no more than a crumb.

The next moment he was out the door. I snatched up warm clothes and hastily put a meal of beans, salt pork, and cornbread upon the table. If White Hawk was so hungry, I reasoned, there must be hunger at L'Arbre Croche as well. By the time I had filled two baskets with food White Hawk was back. He glanced approvingly at the baskets. While I ran to check on Belle and assure her that I would return in a few days, White Hawk, with the hunger of a wolf, ate the dinner I had set for him.

By midmorning we were paddling through the icy waters. The bright sun, the work of paddling, and the fur-lined gloves White Hawk gave me all helped to keep me warm. An occasional gull dropped down to snatch a small fish. In the far distance we could see white slabs of ice moving slowly through the water. Along the shore spring buds on the branches of the maple trees made a pink haze. The two of us had often paddled around the island together. Matching strokes easily, we skimmed gracefully over the water's surface, soon leaving behind the last fishermen.

As we paddled there was a rush of chatter between us, for we had three months' telling to get through. "How is Pere Mercier and the MacNeils and the Wests and all the others on the island?" White Hawk wanted to know.

"Pere Mercier is growing forgetful and says the cobwebs in his brain won't disappear until he can get out in his fishing boat. You missed Elizabeth's wedding. Mr. Brandson was very cross at having to purchase new clothes, but Elizabeth said she would not be married to a man dressed as an undertaker. She even fancied him up in a ruffled shirt. Still, I believe they suit one another very well. Mr. Brandson's only unhappiness is with Mr. Astor's company. There are rumors that the trappers have had a bad year. To find animals they have to go farther west and north. The tribes they have been dealing with all these years can't supply enough pelts. Many of the tribes have sold their hunting lands or have had them taken away by white people greedy for land."

White Hawk said, "It is no different here in the Michigan territory. A Chippewa from the Saginaw area was at L'Arbre Croche. He said Governor Cass is after the Chippewa to sign over their land. It is the same at L'Arbre Croche. With so much hunger it has been all I can do to keep the chiefs holding out against the government's promises of money and food. Now what of your school? I saw happy faces on all your students."

I needed no encouragement to boast about the advances made by my four pupils. "I am proudest of Leah, who has mastered reading. Her father came to complain that she was doing her lessons when she ought to have been helping with the chores. He pounded his fist on my table and shouted, 'Reading and writing will get no farm work done!' He told me he couldn't read and still he had a successful farm. Just the next week the fur company presented their contract to him for this year's crop of beans. Leah read it, for she reads everything she can get her hands on. She pointed out to her father that the contract said the company might cancel their order as late as the middle of summer, long after her father had planted his crop. He had the contract changed. After that there were no more complaints about Leah's learning to read."

And so we talked away as we paddled, remembering to keep an eye out for any patches of ice. When it grew dark we drew close to the shore for safety. It was in the darkness that White Hawk dared to say, "When will our wedding be, Mary? You said in the spring, and spring is here."

"We'll be married in June when the spring planting is done and the lilacs are out. And, White Hawk," I ventured, "you'll stay on the island after we're married?"

White Hawk answered me solemnly. "Ask me again after our visit to my people."

With that I had to be satisfied. Two hours after nightfall we saw our first bonfires. The forest seemed alight.

"They're boiling syrup," White Hawk said. "They've been collecting sap from the maple trees all week. The season was late this year, so the whole camp is at work to make up for lost time. I don't suppose we'll get much sleep tonight."

The women were tending the bonfires under

the kettles of boiling syrup. It was an endless task, for every batch of syrup had to boil for twenty-four hours. The men had cut wood for the fires and hemlock branches. When the syrup threatened to boil over the women dipped a hemlock branch into the kettle. The coolness of the branch settled the boiling syrup. I knew the syrup would be made into maple sugar and sold on the island. To get the many pounds of sugar, thousands of gallons of sap would be boiled for countless hours. The sugar would fetch six or seven cents a pound.

I was so fascinated with the bubbling syrup and with its tempting fragrance that it was several minutes before I looked more closely at the women. What I saw startled me. Like White Hawk's, their faces were pinched and thin. They looked like scarecrows dressed in ill-fitting garments. As sweetly scented as the syrup was, I knew it would offer little nourishment.

When the chief and his wife came to greet me I saw that they, too, were lean and almost feeble. Shocked, I said, "You're not well, Chief Black Kettle."

"It is nothing," the chief said. "It is only that food has been scarce. The deer are hiding in the cedar swamps where we can't follow. Our fishermen have been out, but the fish are lazy in the cold water and will not come to the nets. I am sure you will bring us good luck. Tomorrow will be a better day."

As he left me at Chief Black Kettle's teepee, White Hawk said, "I would have spared you the sad sight of so much hunger, Mary, for I know your kind heart and I know you will be hurt by it. It's this cruel hunger and all the needs of my people that take me so often from Michilimackinac. You asked me before whether I would always stay on the island. I wanted you to understand why I can't say yes to you. I will have to leave the island, but I promise always to return."

Lying awake that night in Chief Black Kettle's teepee, I told myself I did understand. I had to admit that just as I loved my farm and the island, so White Hawk loved his people. The circle that our life together would make would have to be large enough to take in all that we cared for. I would miss White Hawk when he left the island, but I was sure our feelings for one another would stretch as far as he traveled.

In the morning I followed Black Kettle's daughter, Nightbird, and her husband, Spotted Feather, into the woods to collect sap from the maple trees. They spoke no English, but the work was simple and I quickly understood what needed to be done. Spotted Feather balanced a yoke on his shoulders. Hanging from the yoke were two large birch bark pails. Smaller birch bark pails were suspended from basswood spouts that had been pounded into the maple trees. Nightbird and I emptied the smaller pails into the larger ones. We had nearly filled the second of Spotted Feather's pails when we heard shouts from the village. I didn't know what the shouts meant, but I saw Nightbird and her husband exchange a look of joy. They began to run toward the village, the pails on either end of Spotted Feather's yoke swinging wildly so that a trail of sap was left behind him.

When we reached the village I saw that everyone—men, women, and children—was armed with sticks and clubs. Crying out in excitement, they rushed off. The women watching the boiling kettles remained at their posts, but they looked longingly after the people who were now rapidly disappearing into the woods.

Alarmed, I turned to White Hawk, who stood holding a club at arm's length as if it were a poisonous snake. "What is it? Are they going to fight some other tribe? What are you doing with a club?"

White Hawk shrugged his shoulders. In an unhappy voice he said, “The tribe is going to do battle with a bird.”

My mouth dropped open. “All those clubs for one bird?”

“Not one bird, but thousands.”

At last I understood. “Someone has seen passenger pigeons.”

“Yes. They have been seen near here, and men have been out hunting for their roosting grounds.” White Hawk sighed. “At last the tribe’s hunger will be over, but I can’t rejoice at the slaughter. I wish I could stay away, but it will be thought strange if I don’t do as they do.”

I began to follow White Hawk, but he shook his head. “I think you should stay here, Mary. It won’t be a pretty sight.”

But I was too curious to stay behind. I had seen flocks of passenger pigeons on the island and heard stories of their flying overhead in such numbers that they looked like great feathered rivers. But nothing prepared me for what I saw. The roosting grounds made me gasp. It looked as though a terrible wind had come through the woods. The weight of thousands of roosting pigeons had broken the branches off the trees, scattering them over the ground. Branches that weren't already broken off were being hacked away, the better to get at the pigeons' nests, for the young squabs in the nests were thought to be the best tasting.

White Hawk walked slowly into the flailing crowd. Spotted Feather, seeing me standing there alone, showed me how to push at a nest so that it would tumble out of the tree onto the ground. The parents of the young nestlings dove at us, fluttering their wings and squawking in a most pitiful way. Spotted Feather paid them no attention. He picked up the young birds that had fallen and, twisting their necks, tossed them into his basket and hurried on to the next tree. I didn't follow him. I didn't want to twist a lot of little birds' necks.

The ground was covered with bird droppings, and I could hardly walk for slipping. I would have run away, but Spotted Feather handed me a stick. I didn't want him to think me a coward, so I reached up and struck half-heartedly at a nest, which toppled out of the tree. I reached for a squab, telling myself it was no different than twisting the necks of chickens, which I had done many times. Spotted Feather smiled and nodded his approval.

Soon, like everyone else, I was knocking

down the nests and throwing the squabs into a basket. I stopped thinking about the droppings and about what I was doing. I concentrated on thinking of the people's hunger and on seeing how many squabs I could get. Driven out of their nests, the terrified, squawking pigeons were fluttering everywhere and banging into one another.

In one bloody hour it was over. The last pigeon escaped into the sky. The Indians compared notes to see who had the most birds in their baskets. White Hawk came by, carrying a basket heavy with pigeons. Proudly I showed him how many I had.

He nodded. "You've done well."

His tone didn't sound like he meant his words as a compliment. I looked up at him and saw that his mouth was set in a tight line.

"What is it?" I asked. "Surely these pigeons mean the end of the cruel hunger."

"I wish we hadn't been a part of this, Mary," he said. "I know these pigeons will keep my people from hunger, but that's not true for you and me. We have enough food without this killing."

"But White Hawk, there are so many pigeons. Thousands and thousands of them."

"That was once said of other animals around here, and now many have all but disappeared."

In the evening the pigeons and squabs were roasted and devoured by everyone. I made a pretense of eating to be mannerly, but now all I could think about was the baby birds chirping in their nests and all the necks I had wrung. The pigeons that were not eaten would be preserved by being smoked over a slow fire. The threat of hunger for the people of L'Arbre Croche was over.

Before we parted for the night I asked White Hawk to promise that we would leave the next morning. "Belle will be having her calf any day, and I must be there."

"I would rather wait a day or two. A west wind has started up."

"White Hawk, you promised."

White Hawk nodded and said no more.

An hour before dawn White Hawk moved silently into the teepee and woke me. I followed him outside, tiptoeing carefully around the others, who were still asleep, their hunger gone for the first time in many weeks. A fire smoldered in the middle of the teepee. Black Kettle's family all lay with their feet close to the warmth. In the night one of the dogs had crept into the teepee for shelter. Now the dog shook itself and followed us out of the teepee and down to the shore.

"We'll have to leave at once," White Hawk said. "The wind is rising. If it shifts to the north we may see ice drifting our way." I could see that the wind was ruffling the tops of the hemlock trees and sending small waves lapping against the shore.

We settled into the canoe and pushed off with no one to bid us farewell but the women who were keeping the fires burning under the syrup kettles and the little dog that sat on the shore.

The sun rose in the east, blazing out of the icy water and tinting the lake the rosy red of crushed strawberries. A flock of geese, honking and squawking, passed overhead in a precise V. Heading north, they were a sure sign of spring.

Although I had hated the slaughter of the pigeons, by noon the hard work of paddling made me hungry. I couldn't resist the roasted squabs that White Hawk had put in our baskets. After we had eaten them our hands were slippery with grease. We had to wash them off in lake water so cold it made our fingers numb.

By late afternoon, as White Hawk had warned, the north wind started up, sending our canoe skimming over the lake. I was happy to have this assistance, for my arms ached with the paddling, but White Hawk had grown silent and wary. The same sun we had seen flaming the sky in the east was now setting the western sky on fire. When Michilimackinac appeared in the distance I turned to White Hawk with a smile. "We're nearly home," I said, but White Hawk was not looking at the island. Following his gaze I saw a sight that took the breath out of me. Half the lake was covered with ice.

White Hawk cried out to me to paddle hard, and we just managed to steer the canoe away from a floating island of ice headed toward us. Once again we had open water around us. The island grew closer. There were people on the shore, their arms raised in greeting—or warning. They were calling to us, but we couldn't make out the words.

"On your left, Mary!" White Hawk shouted. A gigantic block of ice was cutting us off from the shore. Now we were caught between two fields of ice. Desperately we pushed our paddles against the ice. We might as well have tried to push away a whole continent. The two islands of ice drifted closer and closer, trapping us between them. I snatched my legs away seconds before the ice crushed the bow of the canoe.

"Get out of the canoe, Mary, quickly!" I

dropped my paddle and scrambled up onto the ice, sliding and falling on its slippery, uneven surface. White Hawk was at my side, holding on to me. The next moment we heard the sickening sound of the canoe collapsing as the two sheets of ice collided, tearing the fragile birch bark into shreds.

It was growing darker. Clinging to one another, we stumbled on toward land. The surface of the ice was pocked with holes and covered with humps and ridges, so that we stumbled and fell again and again. I wanted to tell White Hawk how sorry I was for coaxing him to leave L'Arbre Croche. I fell again. I tried to stand, but my legs would not hold me. White Hawk picked me up in his arms and set off. There was no way of knowing how far toward the shore the ice extended. We might find ourselves facing open water.

We heard shouts. Someone was calling to us. I recognized Jacques's voice. His cries were coming closer and closer. Suddenly he appeared only a few feet from us.

"Mary, White Hawk, come quickly. Any moment this ice will break off and float away, and we will go with it. We're not far from shore, and I have a rope fastened to me so we can find our way. White Hawk, let me take Mary." But White

Hawk would not let me go. As Jacques reeled in the rope we followed close behind him, until only a short jump over a sliver of open water set us upon the beach of Michilimackinac.

The whole island had heard of our plight and had gathered along the shore. Even the soldiers from the fort were there. Little Cloud flung her arms around me. Renard hugged my skirts. The MacNeils clucked over us, throwing welcome blankets and shawls about us. Pere Mercier came running from St. Anne's, where he had been praying on our behalf.

I was shivering so from cold and fright that I could not say a word. Dr. West rescued us from the crowd. "You are both suffering from exposure. It's a wonder you didn't freeze to death. We must get you to our house at once, and you, too, Jacques."

When we were settled around the Wests' fire, snug in warm clothes and drinking cups of hot chocolate prepared by Mrs. West, Dr. West said, "You have a brave brother, Mary. His risk of being carried away on the ice was great."

"Nonsense," Jacques said. "There was no bravery at all. It is only that I had to return Mary to the farm. I have no stomach for bringing new calves into the world, and this afternoon Belle had a decidedly maternal look in her eye."

I struggled to my feet. "What if she's having her calf right now! I have to go to her." I found I was weaker than I had thought. Eager as I was to get to Belle, I had to sink down into my chair again.

Dr. West said, "You will do nothing of the kind, Mary. I have delivered a large number of babies, and I don't believe a calf will present a problem. I'll see to Belle."

Mrs. West said, "But Belle is in a barn."

"Yes, my dear," Dr. West replied. "Surely a suitable place for a cow."

"But your clothes, Dr. West!"

"Yes, my dear, you are quite right. I had better change into something more fitting."

"But Dr. West," Mrs. West protested. "You have no clothes proper for a barn."

"I will find something. My old coat has a shine upon it, and there is that pair of breeches a little out at the knees." Moments later, well wrapped in a cloak and carrying a torch, Dr. West was headed out to my farm. When the door had closed upon him, and with only a brief pang of regret for missing Belle's birthing, I fell into a blissful sleep by the fire, White Hawk's hand in mine.

CHAPTER 12

TROUT LILIES, SPRING BEAUTIES, and violets sprang up in the woods, anxious for their day in the sun before the new leaves shaded the forest floor. The eagle perched like a sentinel on its nest. The *voyageurs* and the brigades of traders returned, among them the Gauthiers with a boat full of pelts. At night a hundred bonfires burned in the Indian camp.

I ended school for the year, for it was a busy time on the farm. Beans and cabbage, potatoes and corn, squashes and carrots, onions and parsnips all needed to be planted. The rosemary and lavender plants I had nursed in the cabin all winter had to be settled outside. Belle and her new calf were turned out into the pasture, where I had to watch them closely. They were tired of a diet of moldy hay and parsnip tops and might ruin their digestion with eating too much of the new green grass. The calf would have to be weaned, and butter and cheese made with Belle's milk.

While I worked in the barn and the field, White Hawk worked at building a new room onto the cabin and repairing the chimney. There was much talk as to how the new room was to be formed. I pleaded for a large window so that I might look out at the woods and water, but White Hawk reminded me of the expense of the glass and the winds that would find their way through the windowpanes. But when the window was built, it was the largest one on the island. "A wedding present," White Hawk said.

Our wedding was set for the middle of June. Already the buds on the lilac trees were fat. Little Cloud was to be my maid of honor and Elizabeth my attendant. My students pleaded to be a part of the ceremony. I promised that they might all wear wreaths of flowers in their hair and march into the church after Elizabeth.

The first schooner to land on the island from Detroit had brought a gift from Angelique of a length of the finest white silk for my wedding dress. Mrs. West brought out her fashion books and, together with Elizabeth and Little Cloud, we chose a pattern. "After your wedding, Mary," Mrs. West said, "you can dye the dress a drab color and it will be quite serviceable." I resolved to do nothing of the kind, but to keep the dress for my own daughter.

A letter from Angelique had come with the silk:

My dearest Mary,

How I rejoice for you and White Hawk. How I long to be there for the wedding. On the day of your marriage I will think of you walking down the path from the farm to St. Anne's as I did. I wish you and White Hawk all the happiness Daniel and I have had.

All is well here in our little home in St. John's Wood. Matthew grows taller and sassier day by day. He has won the heart of Mrs. Cunningham, and she spoils him shamelessly.

You will be interested to hear that James and Emma are spending their time between Lindsay House and Castle Oakbridge. I believe the duke and Lady Elinor are quite fond of Emma, as who would not be? She is the means of James's settling down, and she is so gentle and anxious to please. The duke is unwell and is not able to go about in public or to carry out his responsibilities at Castle Oakbridge.

James had an exhibition of his paintings of America. It was all the thing. Everyone talked about the fine scenery in America. I had to laugh when one woman at the exhibition pointed at the portrait of White Hawk and said he was a "handsome savage." James said he was not a savage but a fine scholar, and the woman laughed at James, thinking he was making a jest.

I'm afraid James let his imagination carry him away, for he has a most frightening painting of what appears to be himself, M. and Mme. Gauthier, some burly Frenchmen, and our own Jacques tying up four thugs. Surely Jacques and James would never be a party to such scurrility.

James's painting of little Renard has a place of honor on our mantelpiece. What a fine boy he is. I long for the day when the cousins, Matthew and Renard, may meet.

Though very good things were said about James's work, he tells me that since he returned he is so busy taking over the duke's responsibilities he has no time for sketching or painting. "That part of my life is over," he told me.

The portrait James did of little Matthew, which accompanies this letter, is his last painting. He wished you and White Hawk to have it as a wedding gift.

Mary, dear, you must write to me at once and let me know your wedding plans and the news of the island.

With all my love,
Angelique

I caught my breath as I looked at the portrait and I shed a few tears, for little Matthew, with his black curls and blue eyes, had much of Papa about him. James had put all of his skill into the portrait, so that I would not have been surprised to hear it speak. I sighed at the thought of him giving up painting.

On the island the news was all of Mr. Astor's interest in the far west. He had set up a trading post called Astoria where the great Columbia River empties into the ocean. England and its Northwest Fur Company had once claimed the land for their own. Now England had given it over to America. "Astor and his company will be leaving the island for Astoria before long," Jacques said. "You have to look too hard to find decent pelts in this part of the country. Astor's brigades have cleaned it out."

Even those who had traveled as far west as the Mississippi complained. M. Gauthier said, "I could hardly pay my *engagés* their wages this year. The animals are disappearing, and the Indians are moving farther west." The Gauthiers brought back news that Little Cloud's people in Saukenuk had turned from hunting to farming. "They mean to hold on to their land," Marie Gauthier said. "They have a new leader, Black Hawk, who has been traveling everywhere rallying the other tribes to band together. He is a man who would readily give his life for the land." At this Little Cloud looked frightened, for talk of the giving and taking of lives amongst her people made her unhappy.

There was a rumor on the island that Elizabeth and her husband, Mr. Brandson, might be moving clear across the country with Mr. Astor's company. Mrs. West was beside herself at the thought. "Elizabeth," she wailed, "how will you ever transport all your fine china such a distance?"

We did not like to tell Mrs. West that from all we had heard of life in the wilderness of Astoria, there would be little need for fine china.

At the end of May, Mrs. Sinclair arrived from Detroit on the Bonnarts' sloop. No sooner was her foot upon the solid ground of the island than I found myself crushed in her embrace.

"Oh, Mary, if you only knew how long I had hoped that one day you and my Gavin would be married." I felt her tears against my cheek. "From the moment you were children running about the island together I felt you were meant for one another. If only Mr. Sinclair were here to share my happiness."

There were many visits and parties. Though my mama and papa were not there, Mrs. Sinclair's love and her delight in the coming wedding did much to ease my heart.

On the day of our wedding, a light breeze blew the fragrance of lilacs over the island. The lilacs had come with the French and could be seen in every yard. My own mother had planted lilac shrubs on our farm. I thought she must be smiling as she watched me gather armfuls of flowers to decorate the church from the shrubs she had so lovingly tended.

I carried a bouquet of rare white lilacs as I walked from the farm to the church. Little Cloud guarded my silk skirts against thistles and briars. Renard, his hand in Jacques's, trailed along behind us, stopping every few minutes to examine a beetle or chase a butterfly. When we reached Main Street we found my four pupils, Martha, Aimée, Caroline, and Leah, waiting for us, flowers in their hair and in their hands.

We were nearly to the church when we heard cries of alarm go up. A hundred canoes filled with Indians were making for Michilimackinac. People rushed out of their houses. "It is Chief Pontiac all over again," someone wailed. Many years earlier Pontiac, angry at the British for taking his land, had found his way into the fort and had done away with nearly all the white people on the island. At the sight of the canoes even the Indians who were camped on the island moved restlessly up and down the beach, worried frowns on their faces.

As I stood watching the approaching canoes, and thinking there might be a war instead of a wedding, White Hawk put his hand on my shoulder. When I saw the wide smile on his face, I guessed the truth. He said, "I promised, Mary, that you should have all the Ottawa tribes at L'Arbre Croche to make you a feast for your wedding, and here they are."

They climbed from their canoes dressed in their finest clothes and carrying baskets of food and gifts. Chief Black Kettle led them toward the church. The chief's hair was done in a topknot stuck with eagle and hawk feathers. He wore a long shirt of red calico over his deerskin leggings. Across his shoulder was a beaded and fringed pouch. Spotted Feather had on a British soldier's military coat decorated with bands of gold lace. There were large silver disks in his ears and little brass bells tied around his ankles. Nightbird had a sleeveless deerskin dress embroidered with beads and dyed quills. Her bare arms were circled with bands of silver. The other members of the tribe were as finely dressed, their faces painted yellow and red. It looked as though a flock of brilliantly colored birds had descended upon the island.

They came in such crowds that the small church of St. Anne's could not hold them all. For a moment Pere Mercier looked alarmed at the numbers, but soon he was arranging for a small altar of logs to be thrown together outside of the church. Our wedding took place under a blue sky with half the island and hundreds of Ottawas looking on. After he had spoken the words of the wedding ceremony Pere Mercier surprised us all and pleased our guests by adding the words of the Indian marriage ceremony: "White Hawk and Mary will walk the trail together. White Hawk and Mary will share the same fire."

Afterward a great feast was set out. On one table were fine silver and china and delicate cakes, all the work of Mrs. West. On the other tables were the gifts of the Ottawa, roasted partridge and haunches of venison, baskets of wild strawberries like small rubies, and young cattails cooked in maple syrup.

No one could recall a wedding celebration like ours on the island. M. André and his friends scratched away on their fiddles. White Hawk and I led the dancers, and much to everyone's delight, and to her amazement, Chief Black Kettle led Mrs. West in a series of leaps and whirls.

In the middle of the festivities I saw White Hawk deep in conversation with a Chippewa. When we were together for a moment I asked what the man had said. "There is trouble with

Governor Cass," White Hawk said. "He has made an offer to the Chippewa in the south-eastern part of the territory. He wants six million acres. He is promising all kinds of things in return, and it is rumored he will be taking barrels of whiskey with him for his meeting with the chiefs. The meeting is set for September."

I looked at White Hawk, trying to keep any uneasiness from my expression. "Will you go?" I already knew the answer to my question. I would always have to watch White Hawk come and go. And not just White Hawk. It was in the nature of islands that people would always leave and return.

"I must see what I can do," White Hawk said, "though I don't have much hope. And when I go in the fall, you will go with me." He took my hand. "For now, we'll have the summer on our island."

All that summer we might have been the only two people on the island, and the island all our own.